# ARTEMIS THE HERO

## READ ALL THE BOOKS IN THE GODDESS GIRLS SERIES!

Athena the Brain
Persephone the Phony
Aphrodite the Beauty
Artemis the Brave
Athena the Wise
Aphrodite the Diva
Artemis the Loyal
Medusa the Mean
Goddess Girls Super Special:
The Girl Games
Pandora the Curious
Pheme the Gossip
Persephone the Daring
Cassandra the Lucky
Athena the Proud
Iris the Colorful
Aphrodite the Fair
Medusa the Rich
Amphitrite the Bubbly
Hestia the Invisible
Echo the Copycat
Calliope the Muse
Pallas the Pal
Nyx the Mysterious
Medea the Enchantress
Eos the Lighthearted
Clotho the Fate
Persephone the Grateful
Hecate the Witch
Artemis the Hero

# ARTEMIS THE HERO

JOAN HOLUB & SUZANNE WILLIAMS

Aladdin

NEW YORK LONDON TORONTO SYDNEY NEW DELHI

This book is a work of fiction. Any references to historical events, real people, or real places are used fictitiously. Other names, characters, places, and events are products of the author's imagination, and any resemblance to actual events or places or persons, living or dead, is entirely coincidental.

ALADDIN
An imprint of Simon & Schuster Children's Publishing Division
1230 Avenue of the Americas, New York, New York 10020
First Aladdin hardcover edition December 2022

Also available in an Aladdin paperback edition.

For information about special discounts for bulk purchases, please contact Simon & Schuster Special Sales at 1-866-506-1949 or business@simonandschuster.com.
The Simon & Schuster Speakers Bureau can bring authors to your live event. For more information or to book an event contact the Simon & Schuster Speakers Bureau at 1-866-248-3049 or visit our website at www.simonspeakers.com.
Series designed by Karin Paprocki
Jacket designed by Alicia Mikles
Interior designed by Ginny Kemmerer
The text of this book was set in Baskerville.
Manufactured in the United States of America 1022 FFG
2 4 6 8 10 9 7 5 3 1
Library of Congress Control Number 2022942026
ISBN 9781534457461 (hc)
ISBN 9781534457454 (pbk)
ISBN 9781534457478 (ebook)

*We appreciate our mega-amazing readers!*
*Sammi F., Layla S., Autumn M., Mary Ann B., Andrade Family, Sara L., Emily E., Barbara E., George H., Paul H., Kristen S., Saad S., Debbie R., Jay G., Twila P., Arnie D., Melissa P., Ana R., Anna D., Lorie Ann G., Missy K., Rena W., Ellie V., Kate H., Thea M., Martha Y., Serena B., Althea U., Lucia J., Catalina J., Elena J., Sofia R., E. A., Dawn D., Heather R., Brielle C., Cory C., Danni S., Savannah Q., and you!*
*—J.H. and S.W.*

*For my sweet and heroic grandchildren:*
*Heidi, Louise, and Chuck*
*—S.W.*

*For J.R.H., my mom/hero*
*—J.H.*

# CONTENTS

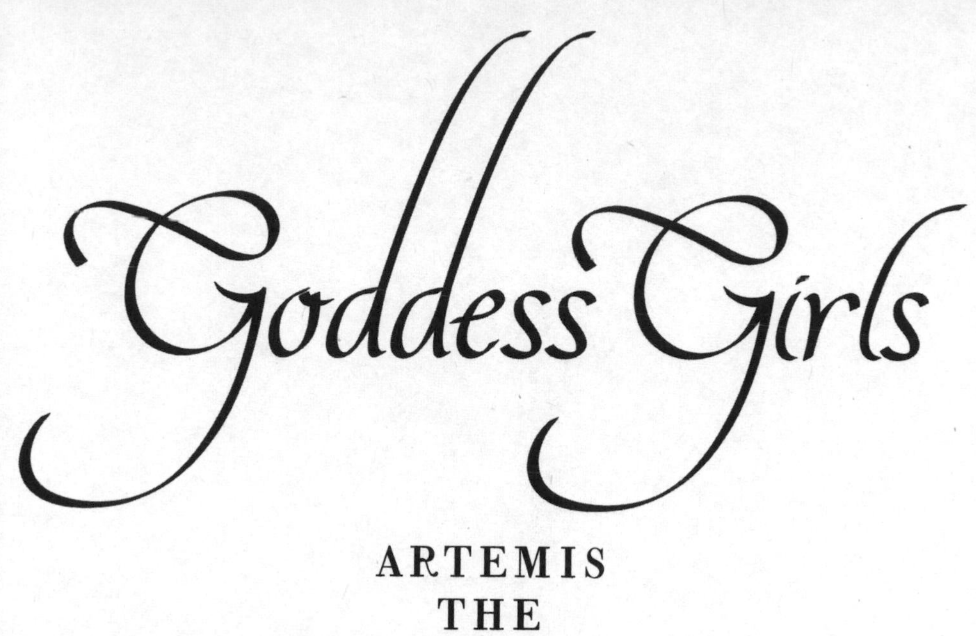


# ARTEMIS THE HERO

# 1
# A Plea for Help

AS SOON AS CLASSES WERE OVER ON FRIDAY afternoon at Mount Olympus Academy, the goddessgirl Artemis rushed upstairs to the girls' dorm on the fourth floor. When she burst into her room, her three dogs wiggled and howled with joy. *Arooo!*

Her greyhound, Nectar, named after the divine

drink that kept Greek goddesses and gods immortal, was especially eager to see her. He leaped to the floor from the crumpled linens atop Artemis's spare bed, where he'd been napping with her other two dogs.

Artemis quickly threw her bag—full of scrolls for classes—onto the bed on the other side of the room as Nectar scrambled over. He began to dance around her. Leaning forward a little, she braced her hands on her thighs. "Can I have a kiss?" she asked him.

The greyhound stood on his hind legs and pushed his front paws against her chest. Then he licked her cheek. Artemis kissed him back on the top of his long nose. "Love you too, boy!"

Dog slobber never bothered her the way it did one of her besties, the goddessgirl Aphrodite. That, plus the mess Artemis and her dogs made, were the main

reasons she and Aphrodite had stopped rooming together some time ago. The two girls' housekeeping styles were just completely different. Artemis took a relaxed approach, whereas Aphrodite was super-duper-mega-neat.

Luckily, the room split hadn't affected their friendship. And they were also BFFs with two awesome goddessgirls named Athena and Persephone. Athena roomed in the girls' dorm too, but Persephone mostly lived off-campus with her mom. When she did spend the night at MOA, she slept in Aphrodite's room.

"Thanks for the kiss," Artemis told Nectar before gently lowering his front paws to the floor. Immediately she was ambushed by Amby (her beagle) and Suez (her bloodhound). The name Amby was short for *ambrosia*, a divine food eaten

by immortals. And Suez—Zeus spelled backward—was named after MOA's formidable principal. Also known as Athena's dad!

Laughing, Artemis kneeled to accept more kisses. "You guys act like you haven't seen me for a century instead of just a few hours." She scratched behind Suez's ears with one hand and rubbed up and down Amby's neck with the other.

After greetings had been thoroughly and happily exchanged, she threaded her way past the mountains of laundry piled here and there on her floor. That morning she'd had to kick through the haphazard stacks of clothes to find a clean chiton to put on for class. The flowing gowns were standard wear for Greek mortal and immortal girls and women. The piles had been here for so long that she hardly noticed them. They were almost like furniture! And

by now it was becoming hard to tell which clothes were clean and which were dirty.

She supposed she'd better wash the whole lot soon. *Sigh.* It wouldn't be that hard, really. It would only require her to do a bit of wash, dry, fold-up, organize, and hang-up magic spells. Still, that would take *some* time, and there were about a million other things she'd rather do! So . . . maybe later.

Stepping over dog toys and old discarded school projects, she finally made it to the far corner of her room. There she bent to check that her dogs still had plenty of food and water. They did. On the way back across the room, she stepped on a doggie squeak toy and stumbled to her knees.

When Artemis stood again, she found herself staring at her reflection in the mirror that hung on the outside of her closet door. She noticed that her

glossy black curls had sprung loose from the gold band that held them together in a simple twist at the back of her head. She slipped the gold band out, gathered her hair high, and re-clasped the band around it.

Then she noticed that her chiton was kind of wrinkly. There were some dirt spots on it too. But they weren't very big. Hardly noticeable, really. Probably happened during third-period Beast-ology class today while she was tracking a winged griffin through a place on Earth called the Forest of the Beasts. She sniffed the chiton's hem. Not completely fresh, but not exactly stinky, either. No reason to change clothes, she decided. She flicked off a piece of dirt and pressed the wrinkles smoother with her palm. There. Grooming done!

"Okay, guys. Ready for your walk?" she asked her three hounds as she turned from the mirror.

They began to bark in reply. Then they ran over to the door and pawed at it.

"Just give me one more minute," Artemis called as she looked around for her favorite archery bow.

Finally she spotted the polished olive-wood bow leaning up against the side of her spare closet. A closet she let Aphrodite use, because that girl had too many chitons to fit in her own two closets. Her wardrobe was enormous, and she often changed outfits several times a day. Artemis couldn't imagine doing that. What a waste of time, when you could be out doing fun stuff with your dogs, practicing archery skills, or playing winged-sandal ball games!

Quickly, Artemis slung the bow over her back.

"Now, where did I leave my quiver?" she muttered, glancing around. Minutes ticked by as she hunted for it through the many piles and stacks of stuff around her room.

Her dogs pawed faster at the door and began to whine. They got like this every morning and afternoon when she returned from classes. They were anxious to get outside to romp and do their bathroom business!

"Sorry! I'm hurrying, I'm hurrying," Artemis told them as she frantically dug under a pile of textscrolls atop her desk. Meanwhile, the dogs were becoming more frenzied. "Ye gods! You guys must really need to pee! Hold on just another sec."

At last she unearthed the tooled leather quiver that held her silver arrows and slung it across her back next to her bow. She and her twin brother,

Apollo, who were both thirteen, were the school's best archers. And, except for when she attended classes, she rarely went anywhere without her bow and arrows. Because you never knew when archery equipment might come in handy.

As goddessgirl of the hunt (as well as the forest and the moon), she served as the protector of animals, nymphs, and other creatures who dwelled in the forests. Hers was a big job, considering she also had to go to classes and keep her grades up, plus find time to hang out with her friends and do sports. No wonder she had no time to clean!

"Finally!" she said, rushing to her three hounds. The dogs barked and wagged their tails. "Okay, okay. Sorry about the wait. I'm sure it felt like forever to you guys, but it wasn't really. We can go now."

The second she opened the door, Nectar, Amby,

and Suez zoomed down the dorm hallway ahead of her, their nails clicking against the floor. At the end of the hall, she pushed out through the door onto the landing. A few godboys passed her as she started downstairs. They mumbled "hi" and "howsitgoing" before continuing up to the boys' dorm on the fifth floor. As she and her hounds continued down the marble staircase to the Academy's entrance, they passed more students on their way up to their rooms.

Several paused to pet the dogs before continuing on up, but Artemis tried to keep moving. They were on a time-critical mission. As in—Mission Dog Bathroom!

Since there weren't a lot of pets at MOA, Amby, Nectar, and Suez always got a lot of attention. The few other animals here included Zeus's famous magical, white-winged horse, Pegasus, and a cute

black-and-white kitten named Adonis. Aphrodite and Persephone shared the care of the kitten. But since Adonis mostly liked to stay in their room, other students didn't see him as much they did Artemis's dogs.

After reaching the bottom of the staircase, Artemis rushed her dogs through the Academy's massive bronze front doors. Happy to be outside at last, they raced ahead of her down a set of sparkling granite steps to the marble courtyard below. She hurried to catch up with them, knowing they'd be anxious to get to the trail beyond it.

"Hey, Artemis! Wait up!" someone called. She turned to spy a mortal boy with light brown hair and gray eyes. Actaeon! He peeled off from his friends and crossed the courtyard toward her. Her brother, Apollo, plus Poseidon, Hades, and some other godboys, watched him head her way.

On hearing Actaeon's voice, Suez skidded to a halt. Changing direction, he joyfully raced over to the mortal boy and barreled into him.

Actaeon laughed, stumbling back a step under the dog's weight. "Hey there. Glad to see you, too." Squatting down, he ruffled the fur on Suez's neck. Unwilling to be left out, Amby and Nectar were soon leaping around him as well.

Watching Actaeon, Artemis felt a familiar fluttery feeling in her chest. Against all odds—especially considering that she'd only really gotten to know him after she'd lost her temper and transformed him into a deer a while back—this boy had become her crush. The two of them shared a love of archery and dogs. Aside from that, she liked how good-natured, kind, fun, and funny he was. Plus, he was cute!

Smiling, she caught up to him. "Too bad my dogs

don't like you," she joked as Amby rolled over to let Actaeon rub his belly, and Nectar nuzzled the boy's free hand.

Her crush grinned at her. "You guys going for a walk?"

"Mm-hm. Want to come? Fair warning, we're kind of in a hurry, though," she told him. If her dogs didn't get to the trail soon, at least one of them was going to have an accident right here in the courtyard. She definitely didn't need that to happen in front of Actaeon. It would be majorly embarrassing!

Impatient for more of the boy's attention, Suez pushed in front of Nectar. Laughing, Actaeon stroked behind the bloodhound's big droopy ears.

"Sorry, can't," he told Artemis. Still kneeling, he cocked his thumb back toward his friends, saying,

"Your brother, Hades, Poseidon, me, and some other guys are heading off to Game On! in a few."

Game On! was this incredible gaming store that had recently opened up in the Immortal Marketplace, which was located halfway between Earth and Mount Olympus. The IM had dozens and dozens of cool shops under its high-ceilinged crystal roof. In Artemis's humble opinion, though, Game On! was the coolest. It had a sunken arena divided into three play areas. And she had helped design the very first game played at its grand opening!

Trying to hide her disappointment, Artemis shrugged. When her dogs blasted off for the trail, she began backing away from Actaeon and moving after them. "That's okay. But I kind of need to get going, so . . ."

She sometimes wished she and Actaeon spent

more time together. Like Aphrodite and Persephone did with their crushes, Ares and Hades. On the other hand, she did value her independence and also liked having plenty of time for her pets, sports, and friends.

Perhaps sensing her disappointment, Actaeon called, "Can we meet up in the cafeteria later? Maybe go drink some shakes at the Supernatural Market after dinner?"

Her heart lifted. "Sure!" When he stood up, she thought about dashing back to him to give him a kiss on the cheek. Only she'd never kissed a boy before. He'd kissed *her* on the cheek once, but that was ages ago. And this probably wasn't the best time, anyway, with his friends looking on. To tell the truth, she never felt like she knew how to act around him.

Actaeon was only her second crush ever. Her first

crush—a mortal actor named Orion—had been a total disaster. Though she hadn't been able to see it at the time, he'd been way too full of himself to care about anyone else.

"Later, then." With a wave of his hand, Actaeon pivoted and went to rejoin his friends.

As Artemis jogged across the courtyard after her dogs, she reflected that another reason she liked Actaeon so much was because of how *un*like Orion he was. She just wished she felt more sure of herself around him. But despite growing up with a twin brother and hanging out with guys in sports, she'd never been able to figure boys out. Not when it came to crushes, anyway.

Within minutes she'd caught up with her hounds at a small grove of olive trees to one side of the courtyard. These silver-green trees had sprung up after

Athena invented the olive as a science-fair project when she'd first come to the Academy. She was the brainiest of Artemis's BFFs. Pretty much the brainiest immortal student at MOA, in fact. There were many other inventions to her credit besides the olive—ships, flutes, plows, and crafts, too.

After passing through the olive grove, Artemis and her dogs moved onto a trail that wound along a river and would eventually circle her back to the olive grove. It was a three-mile loop—the perfect length for exercise. As usual, she paused now and then along the trail to let her dogs wander off a ways and do their bathroom business.

Since very few paths forked off from this trail, there was little chance they'd get lost. However, Artemis tried to pay careful attention to their whereabouts and her surroundings at all times. She could

get lost just about *anywhere*. For as long as she could remember, her sense of direction had been awful. As Apollo liked to tease, she was so directionally challenged that she probably couldn't find her way out of a papyrus bag!

When her dogs were finally finished with their business and ready to romp, Artemis called to them, and they continued their walk at a faster pace. They were about halfway around the loop when her stomach began to growl with hunger. Luckily, she always brought snacks.

"Just a sec!" she called to her dogs. Stopping by the side of the trail, she leaned her bow against a big rock and shrugged off her quiver. She pulled out her three magical silver arrows—a gift from her goddessgirl friends on her and Apollo's thirteenth birthday—then dug around inside the quiver. At the

very bottom, she located a Bite o' Heaven ambrosia bar. She also found the bag of dog treats she kept there. So, before peeling the wrapper from her ambrosia bar, she tossed a handful of bone-shaped biscuits toward her hounds. They scrambled to get them and scarfed them down lickety-split.

Just as quickly, she devoured her snack bar, then shoved her arrows back inside her quiver. "Okay, boys. Let's keep going," she said, swinging both quiver and bow across her back. But they'd only just begun to walk again when a feeling of unease came over her and she went still.

*Uh-oh!* Was Apollo in some kind of trouble? She and her brother could sometimes pick up on each other's feelings long-distance. And when they did, they paid attention.

Artemis squeezed her eyes shut and concentrated

on seeing him in her mind's eye. Slowly, she recited a chant she and Apollo had made up in childhood: "Come, my twin, give me a clue—a picture I can use to find you!" They'd been born with a special twin sense: the ability to locate each other in this way, as long as the other twin was willing to be found.

Right away a picture swam into her head. She saw a tall, arched entrance inside the Immortal Marketplace, carved with fancy scrollwork entwined with figures of the goddesses and gods of Mount Olympus. They were engaged in a stunning battle against the giant Titans in a long-ago war called the Titanomachy. It only took her a moment or two to realize that what she was seeing was actually the entrance to Game On!

Of course! Apollo was one of the guys Actaeon had just gone there with. She tried to locate both

her brother and her crush within the image she'd conjured up, but the picture faded too fast. Well, at least she knew that Apollo must be fine, since he'd obviously made it to where he'd been going.

So why did she still feel uneasy?

As she continued down the trail, her dogs bounded ahead of her. Alongside them, the fast-moving river tumbled over rocks as it flowed down the mountain-side. Suddenly she noticed rustling and sighing sounds in the trees she was passing. Yet no wind stirred their branches.

A shiver ran down her spine. Something was definitely up.

Just then, a lovely, clear voice called out to her. "Artemis, most worthy of goddesses. Protector of all who dwell in the forests. A nymph has need of your help!"

"Pitys? Is that you?" Artemis called out, turning in a circle. She'd recognized the voice as belonging to one of the nymphs who lived among the trees along this part of the trail.

Sure enough, Pitys shyly parted the leaves of a nearby tree to peek out at her. One by one, three more pale faces, glowing like fairy lights, peeped from behind tree trunks and in between branches. Then the four nymphs, each around Artemis's age, swung down to land in her path.

# 2
## Boy Trouble

"WHO AMONG YOU NEEDS HELP?" ARTEMIS asked, glancing in concern from one nymph to the other as they gathered around her.

These nymphs were all graceful, slightly taller than her, and slim . . . in other words, *willowy*. (Even though they didn't actually live in willow trees.) Leaves were woven into their hair, and they wore gowns decorated

with bark and vines. Not only were their outfits cute, but they also served as camouflage, allowing them to blend into the forest whenever the need arose. The nymphs seldom wore sandals, but instead wove flowers around their ankles and the toes of their bare feet. To Artemis's relief, they all looked unhurt.

"Well?" she prodded when none of them spoke right away. Though her concern for them was making her heart beat fast, she kept her voice calm. She liked the fact that the nymphs all looked up to her and considered her their protector. She never wanted them to lose faith in her. But she worried they might if she acted uncertain or didn't seem to be in control when faced with a tricky situation.

"What's up?" Artemis prompted again as Amby, Nectar, and Suez ran over and sniffed at the nymphs' gowns. Accustomed to animals, since many

dwelled in their forest, the nymphs happily petted and hugged them.

"I'm so glad we found you," Pitys said finally as the dogs wandered off a short distance to explore new scents. Though her voice sounded serene, her face appeared troubled. Artemis waited patiently for her to go on. Usually, nymphs bounced and twirled with joy, but they could quickly become distressed and shy if pressed too hard.

To further put them at ease, Artemis pointed to Pitys's outfit, a stunning buttercup-yellow chiton decorated with laurel leaves, berries, and flowers. And this nymph's favorite—fresh-smelling pine needles. "Is that one of Echo's designs?" Artemis asked.

Pitys perked up at the question, spinning to show off the chiton. "Yes, I picked it up this morning from the Immortal Marketplace."

Echo was another tree nymph, one well-known for the woodland fashions she created. As everyone knew, the famous fashion designer Moda had taken her on as an apprentice recently. When not studying with him, Echo lived in a sweet tree house in the forested mountains of Boeotia, Greece. Her fashion ideas sprang from nature, and she often used forest materials in her designs.

"Cool," Artemis replied. "She's super talented and—"

"Enough about Echo and her designs. Arethusa needs help!" a nymph with short cherry-red hair burst out impatiently. Her name was Britomartis, but when Artemis had made the mistake of calling her that once, she'd practically exploded. "I hate my real name!" the touchy nymph had declared. "Call me Dicte!" She'd chosen the nickname herself, liking

that it was the name of the mountain in Crete where Zeus had been born. Ever since then, Artemis had tried to remember to call her by that name.

At last, here was a hint about why these four had come out to greet her! If one of the nymphs was in trouble, that would explain the unease Artemis had felt earlier. It had been caused by something going on with Arethusa, not by Apollo at all.

Though the bond Artemis shared with her nymph friends was not as strong as the bond she shared with her twin brother, it was still powerful. She cared for all nymphs in nature, whether they dwelled in woods, water, mountains, or even the clouds. So when any were in distress, she sensed it, even if she couldn't identify exactly who needed her help.

Artemis liked Arethusa a lot, and they'd hunted

together many times. Though shy around those she didn't know well, the nymph was sweet and good-natured. Unless she was upset. Then she could become a bit of a drama queen.

"Brit—um, I mean *Dicte*, what's happened to Arethusa? Where is she?" Artemis asked, her forehead creasing with worry. Her eyes darted around the forest, trying to catch sight of Arethusa, as her mind raced with dreadful possibilities. Had she fallen down a cliff or out of a tree and broken a leg or something? She was a sea nymph, and so wasn't all that great at climbing.

"C'mon, what kind of trouble is she in?" Artemis demanded, growing more impatient and worried when the nymph didn't answer at once.

"*Boy* trouble," Dicte replied at last. Her face turned a bit pink as the four nymphs exchanged a

look. Nymphs had a reputation for being boy crazy, but it wasn't exactly fair. They were no more boy crazy than the average goddessgirl or mortal girl, in Artemis's humble opinion. Which was to say they had plenty of other interests. Indeed, many of them hardly gave boys a thought.

Pitys pointed down to the river alongside the trail they all stood on. "Do you know Alpheus? The godboy of this river? He doesn't go to MOA, but he's a friend of Poseidon's."

"Sorry, I don't," Artemis said, shaking her head. "I know Poscidon, though. He does go to MOA." That trident-wielding godboy of the sea was mega-skilled at designing fountains and waterworks. Plus, he often played drums in Heavens Above, her brother's band. And right now he was with Actaeon at Game On!, of course.

The fact that Alpheus, a godboy, didn't attend MOA wasn't at all strange. Though most students at the Academy were goddessgirls and godboys, not *all* goddessgirls and godboys attended the school. You had to be lucky enough to receive an invitation from Zeus to enroll.

Putting two and two together, Artemis said, "I'm guessing this Alpheus is the source of Arethusa's boy trouble?"

The nymphs all nodded. "He has a *huge* crush on Arethusa," Dicte told Artemis, her eyes going wide as she said the word "huge."

"But she doesn't like him back," called Karya, the third nymph on the path. This chestnut-haired nymph had been playing with Artemis's dogs, but now she ran over to chime in on the discussion. "Not

like that, anyway. I don't know why, though. *I* think he's dreamy!"

"*Fig*ures," said Syke, who was the nymph of fig trees. "But that's only because you're *nuts*," she teased affectionately.

Karya giggled and twirled in a quick circle, while the other nymphs laughed. She *was* the nymph of nut trees. In fact, a chestnut earring dangled from one of her earlobes right now, and a walnut earring hung from the other.

"Go on. About Arethusa?" Artemis prodded.

"Oh, right. Well, she made the mistake of taking a drink from Alpheus's river this morning," Pitys continued. "She was out running along the trail and got thirsty."

Dicte scowled. "When Alpheus caught Arethusa

drinking without permission, he took away the cup she was using—her special wooden drinking cup. Her father carved it for her when she was a baby, so of course she wants it back!"

"Besides that, it's magical," Karya piped up to add. "Arethusa told me so!" She giggled again. "I wonder if the cup's magic could help it do a move like this!" With that she turned a quick series of cartwheels. These nymphs could never stand still for long!

The others were all staring at her when she landed upright. "What?" Karya asked in confusion.

"Her cup is *magical*?" Pitys scoffed, crossing her arms. "How so? I've never heard her say that."

Dicte frowned at Karya. "Me neither."

"Nor me," said Syke.

Karya's eyes went wide. "Oops. I forgot. She

told me it was a secret." She put a finger to her lips. "Shh." Then she giggled again.

*Of all Arethusa's nymph friends, why would she choose to tell Karya something she wanted kept secret?* Artemis wondered as she watched the nymph do a handstand. This giggly girl was the absolute worst at keeping secrets.

According to Syke, when the nymphs had planned a party for Pitys on her last birthday, Karya had blurted their plans to Pitys ten minutes after they'd made them! "What part of '*surprise* birthday party' didn't you understand?" Dicte had apparently asked Karya in exasperation.

No, it just didn't make sense that Arethusa would have trusted Karya with such a secret. Probably Arethusa had just been joking around. The other nymphs must have thought so too, because they didn't

bother to press Karya for details about the cup's supposed "magic." (Though if it did have a magic ability, Artemis doubted it would be cartwheeling!)

"So anyway, Arethusa told us she begged Alpheus to give her cup back," Pitys said, picking up the story again.

"But he said he'd only return it if she promised to give him something in trade, and she agreed without asking what he wanted," said Syke. She made a tsking sound. "Big mistake."

"Yeah," said Dicte, her face going pink again. "It was a trick. Because Alpheus told her he wants her to go out with him!"

"What? You mean like on a *date*?" Artemis asked.

The nymphs all nodded. "And Arethusa doesn't want to," said Pitys.

Artemis frowned. "Then she shouldn't. No girl or

boy should ever be tricked into doing something like that if they don't want to do it."

"We agree," Dicte said gravely. "But breaking a promise to a god, even a minor river god like Alpheus, can have terrible consequences."

*That's true,* thought Artemis. Goddesses and gods were entitled to take revenge for disrespectful actions, including promises made to them and later broken. Even her friend Athena, who seldom got truly angry, had once turned a mortal girl into a spider for disrespecting Zeus. The girl's name was Arachne, and she'd dared to weave a tapestry that showed Athena's illustrious dad foolishly wounding himself in the foot with one of his own thunderbolts!

"You know how Arethusa can be sometimes. Scared at the drop of a leaf. She likely made the promise while too upset to think straight," said Syke.

The other three nymphs nodded, and then they all gazed at Artemis as if expecting her to immediately announce a plan to resolve this tangle. Huh? She didn't have one! Boy trouble was more Aphrodite's department than hers. Aphrodite was the goddess of love, after all. However, she wasn't here, and these nymphs were depending on Artemis for help.

"Poor Arethusa," Artemis murmured. Surely there was more to this story than what she'd learned so far. "Where is she right now?" she asked the nymphs.

"Hiding," Karya said matter-of-factly.

Pitys nodded. "She does that when she's upset."

"Okay," said Artemis, trying to be patient. "But where exactly is she hiding?"

"At the bottom of the well," said Dicte. All four nymphs pointed to a path that led to a quaint old

stone well that had been abandoned years ago after its water ran dry.

"I'll go talk to her," Artemis said. When the nymphs started to follow her, she added, "Alone."

"That's probably best," Syke remarked to the other nymphs. "You know how skittish she can get with a lot of people around."

"Right," said Artemis. "Oh, and could you all watch my dogs while I'm gone, please?" The dogs were now clustered around the trunk of a large fir tree near the trail, staring up into its branches and barking. A big gray squirrel was chittering back at them.

"Sure," said Karya, perking up.

"Yeah. We'll throw some sticks for them," said Syke. "We just trimmed some of our trees' branches, so there are plenty around."

While the nymphs went to play with her dogs, Artemis took the path to the old well. Once she reached it, she could see that its wooden cover had been pulled off and tossed aside. She leaned over and looked inside, but she couldn't see to the bottom. However, there was a rope ladder that went down into the deep dark hole.

"Arethusa-sa-sa?" she called, her voice echoing down the well. "Are you down there-ere-ere?"

# 3
## Arethusa

AT FIRST THERE WAS NO ANSWER. THEN Arethusa's voice came echoing up the sides of the old well. "Pitys? Syke? Is that you? Go away, please. I—I don't want to see anyone."

"It's me, Artemis. If you'll come up and talk to me, maybe I can help you."

"Artemis?" A note of relief came into the nymph's

voice. “Hold on.” Seconds later she climbed up the ladder and pushed herself out over the edge of the well to stand on the ground.

“Thank godness you’re here,” she said, hugging Artemis tightly. “I’m in a terrible fix and I don’t know what to do about it!” There must have been at least a small amount of water still at the bottom of the well, because the hem of her sky-blue chiton was damp, Artemis noticed. Since this nymph was in charge of a water spring on the Greek island of Ortygia, however, a bit of dampness never bothered her.

After Arethusa released her, Artemis picked up the round wooden cover and quickly slid it in place to seal off the top of the well. She wouldn’t put it past this fraidy-cat nymph to leap back inside if she got at all spooked while they talked over her problem.

That done, Artemis plopped down to sit with her back against the side of the well.

She patted the ground beside her. "Join me," Artemis invited. "Pitys and the others told me some of what happened with Alpheus. Can you fill in the details?"

With a sigh, Arethusa gracefully dropped to sit beside her. "So . . . they told you he tricked me? That he won't give me back my cup unless I go out with him?"

Artemis nodded.

Arethusa's cheeks flamed red. "It's just sooo embarrassing!" she said dramatically. She tossed her head, which made her long, beautiful sea-green hair sway back and forth. "I never should've made that stupid promise without asking what he wanted!"

"Well, yes. It would've been good to know up

front what you were actually promising," Artemis agreed. Before she could add that that didn't excuse Alpheus for tricking her, tears sprang into Arethusa's lovely blue eyes.

"I wasn't thinking!" the girl cried. She began to sob. "I don't want to go on a date with him, but what can I do? I have to get my cup back!"

Artemis put an arm around the girl. "There, there. Don't worry. We'll fix this somehow," she said, patting Arethusa's shoulder awkwardly. It was easy for her to do things like fighting off beasts and battling warriors. But comforting others was not something she felt particularly good at. Luckily, the nymph calmed down enough to stop sobbing.

Using her fingertips to brush her tears away, Arethusa said, "Alpheus told me he'll safeguard my cup until I keep my promise. And if I *don't* keep my

promise, he'll claim it as a gift because his birthday is tomorrow. I can't give up my cup, but I *don't* want to go out with that meanie!"

"Don't worry. Not gonna happen, and that's *my* promise to you," Artemis told her firmly. "We'll figure something out."

Arethusa nodded in relief. "I tried to offer him a different trade, like a shell necklace or some seaweed stew, but he refused everything I thought of."

Artemis frowned. "He sounds stubborn."

"Yeah," said Arethusa. "And mega-annoying! He only gave me till five o'clock tomorrow afternoon to keep my promise. Not only that, but he insists our date must happen someplace where others will see us together. We'll meet at the river, and then he wants to go to the Supernatural Market on our date. Can you believe that? How embarrassing! When

time runs out, if I haven't shown up, he said he'll hide my cup somewhere so I'll never find it." New tears trickled down her cheeks. "Oh, Artemis. What should I do?" she moaned dramatically.

Artemis tapped her chin, thinking. "Tell you what," she said at last. "A promise made to an immortal is not something to take lightly. But I'll go talk to him. See if I can convince him to forget the promise you made, maybe in trade for something else besides a necklace or stew."

Arethusa's face brightened at once. "You will?" She hugged Artemis. "You're the best goddessgirl ever!" she exclaimed. "A *hero*, in fact! If we nymphs didn't have you to look after us, I don't know what we'd do!"

*Maybe solve your own problems?* Artemis thought as the nymph clung to her. But she didn't say this

aloud. In truth, the nymphs didn't ask for her help with *every* small difficulty they encountered. They knew she couldn't be around all the time. Still, far too often they contacted her with problems she thought they should've tried harder to fix before involving her.

On the other hand, it was her duty to help this girl. She adored her nymph friends, and part of her goddessgirl role was to protect them. If she succeeded in sorting out this Alpheus problem, it would give her a great feeling of pride and satisfaction. She really did want to be the hero Arethusa and the other nymphs seemed to think she was.

After gently unhooking the nymph's arms from around her neck, Artemis stood up. "I'll go down to the river to look for Alpheus," she said. "Want to come along?"

Arethusa's blue eyes went wide. "Do I have to?" She wrapped her arms around her knees and rocked back and forth. "Couldn't I just stay here?" A frown crept onto her face. "I'm so mad at that godboy I might just kick him. So maybe it wouldn't be a good idea for me to go."

It was clear that this poor nymph was not only angry at the river god, but embarrassed at what she'd gotten herself into. Was she also uneasy about confronting him? Artemis could understand that, actually. She sometimes had a hard time bringing up uncomfortable subjects with others too. "It's okay—you don't have to come," Artemis told the nymph.

"Really? Thank you!" Arethusa jumped to her feet. Then she reached for the wooden well cover and began to tug it off.

"Stop!" said Artemis. "Why hide in that icky, dark,

damp place? Just go hang out in the trees with the other nymphs till I return."

Arethusa beamed at her. "Good idea! You are sooo smart! I'll ask Syke if I can hang out with her."

Together the two girls left the well. When Artemis began to walk along the path in the wrong direction, Arethusa called out, "C'mon. The river's this way!"

Artemis pivoted. "Oh yeah, thanks. I knew that." Although she hadn't! She'd been so caught up in thinking about Arethusa's woes that she'd neglected to pay attention to her surroundings the way she always tried to remember to do.

Once they'd gone halfway up the correct path, Artemis could hear her dogs barking. "Your turn, Amby. Catch it!" Karya's voice rang out.

A second later, Artemis and Arethusa ducked when a stick came their way, hurtling over their

heads to land just beyond them on the main trail.

*Woof! Woof!*

"Look out!" squeaked Artemis when all three of her hounds came tearing after it, almost bowling over her and Arethusa. The dogs stopped short when they saw them, however. Abandoning their game, and having no more sense of time than Artemis did of direction, they leaped on her as if she'd been gone for days instead of minutes.

Artemis laughed. "Down, boys! You just saw me like ten minutes ago."

Quickly, she thanked the nymphs for looking after her dogs. Leaving Arethusa to explain that she'd volunteered to speak to Alpheus, Artemis set off along the trail loop again with Nectar, Suez, and Amby trotting alongside her.

By now they were more than halfway around the

three-mile loop. In another half mile she noticed a spot where the trail dipped down to the banks of the river. This seemed like a good place to call on Alpheus for a little chat. She had no idea what the river god would consider a fair trade for the cup, however.

Hmm. What could a river god use? A new fishing net? A sailboat? A canoe? Floaties? Once they got to talking, she figured he'd say something that would give her an idea for what might interest him.

# 4

# Alpheus

ARTEMIS SOON REACHED THE RIVERBANK. Standing in the shade of some silvery willows, she gazed out over the river's crystal-clear water, which sparkled in the late afternoon sun. The river moved more slowly here than in other places. Its water looked so cool and delicious that she could understand why Arethusa had stopped to dip her cup and drink.

In fact, Artemis's three hounds wasted no time in scrambling down the bank to lap up some of that sweet, cool water. Luckily, the river god wasn't there to see, or he might've demanded something from *them*! After chasing after the sticks the nymphs had thrown, the dogs seemed tired now and lay down in the shade of the willow trees to nap.

They paid no attention when Artemis cupped her hands around her mouth and called out to the river god. "Alpheus? It's Artemis, goddessgirl of the hunt, forest, and moon, and the protector of nymphs. I need to speak with you!"

She cocked her head, listening for a reply. But all she heard was the wind whistling through the willows and the river gurgling as it flowed over rocks. After a bit, she tried again. "Alpheus? Are you near?"

Abruptly, about ten feet out from the bank and

directly across from where Artemis stood, the water began to swirl. Soon it formed a large whirlpool. Up from its center rose the river god himself! He was thin, with turquoise eyes like Poseidon's. He looked about Artemis's age.

"Hiya, Artemis!" he said cheerfully. "Nice to meet ya! Getting hunted down by the goddessgirl of the hunt is a new experience. To what do I owe the pleasure?"

Arethusa had called this river god a "meanie." Caught off guard by his jokey, good-natured greeting, Artemis was momentarily speechless.

Silver streaks in Alpheus's bright blue hair glimmered in the sunlight as he splashed toward shore. Before she could regain her voice, the river god noticed her dogs. Immediately, he veered toward them. "Hey, fellas. How are ya?" he said.

Too comfortable and sleepy to get to their feet, the three hounds lifted their heads as he came near. They eyed him a little warily. But after he sank down beside them and began to ruffle the fur on their necks, they lowered their heads and stretched contentedly.

"I've always wanted a dog. Can't have one of my own, though. I couldn't take care of it, since I spend so much time in this river," Alpheus remarked as Artemis went over to stand near him. "What're their names?"

"Well, the smallest is Amby," Artemis began, remaining wary of this powerful boy. "He's a beagle. Nectar is the skinny greyhound, and Suez is a bloodhound." As she spoke, she pointed to each in turn.

"Suez?" Alpheus laughed in delight. "That's Zeus spelled backward!"

Artemis nodded at him. "Got it in one. Good work. Not many people figure that out right away."

To her surprise, especially after what Arethusa had said about him, this river god was growing on her. Anyway, how could anyone who liked dogs be all bad? Maybe he'd only been teasing when he'd told Arethusa he wouldn't return her cup till she went out with him. Maybe she had run away before he could explain and give back her cup. Thinking this, Artemis said, "I just came from seeing a nymph friend of mine."

"Yeah?" said Alpheus as he scratched Amby behind the ears. "Which one?"

"Arethusa," said Artemis. Was it just her imagination, or did Alpheus go a little stiff when she mentioned the girl's name? She sank down to sit near him, while her dogs snoozed away between them.

“You have something that belongs to her,” she went on. “A wooden cup? Her father carved it for her when she was a baby, so it’s very special to her.”

Talking about the cup reminded her that she’d meant to ask Arethusa if there was any truth to Karya’s insistence that it was magical. Well, she certainly wouldn’t suggest to Alpheus that it might be. That would only make him want to keep it all the more!

“Yep, she told me that about her dad, actually.” Alpheus smiled. “And I *will* return it to her—”

“Oh, thank godness!” Artemis interrupted him to say. “She’ll be so relieved.” Hurrying on, she added, “So if you’ll just give the cup to me, I’ll see that she gets it back.”

“Wait,” Alpheus said, holding his hand up, palm out. “I didn’t finish what I was saying. I’ll return the

cup to Arethusa, *if* she follows through on her promise by five o'clock tomorrow as agreed."

Artemis stared at him, as thunderstruck as if Principal Zeus had zapped her with one of his thunderbolts. "But that's just *mean*! Arethusa doesn't want to go out with you. She doesn't really know you or *like* you!"

"She d-doesn't?" Now it was Alpheus's turn to look thunderstruck. "Then why did she drink from my river?" he asked, sounding confused.

Artemis rolled her eyes. "Godsamighty. You can't think that whoever drinks from your river is in *like* with you. My dogs just drank from your river, and they're not!"

With incredibly bad timing, Amby stretched and stood up, then lunged at the still-sitting Alpheus and licked his arm. Artemis couldn't help cracking up.

"I take that back," she said. "Amby *does* seem to be a little bit in like with you."

Alpheus chuckled. "Know what? You're cool, Artemis. I like you. And your dogs!"

Artemis felt herself softening toward him again. "You're cooler than I expected, too. So will you let Arethusa off the hook and—"

"I'll think about it," Alpheus interrupted her to say. He gave each of her dogs one last pat and then stood. "But right now I gotta go check on my river farther downstream. Some trees fell over in a windstorm last night, and I may need to shift them so they don't block the flow."

Artemis stood too. "What about the cup?" She was reluctant to leave without it, but feared that if she pushed too hard, he might simply refuse to cooperate.

Alpheus gave her a cocky grin. "Don't worry. I'm keeping it safe." Then he added, "I'll meet you here at this same spot tomorrow morning. Say, nine o'clock? We can talk more then." With that he spun on his heel, jogged down the bank, and dove into his river. *Splash!*

Well, *that* had been a strange and disappointing meeting!

"Okay, I'll come," Artemis called to him, even though she wasn't sure he'd hear. "But make sure you bring Arethusa's cup with you!"

She waited a few seconds to see if he'd surface and reply. When he didn't, she put two fingers between her lips and whistled to her dogs. As they started up the trail toward MOA again, she glanced upward. Already Helios the sun god and his magnificent chariot were nearing the horizon. Pulled by fiery

horses that breathed out flames, this chariot carried the sun across the sky every day.

"Hurry, boys," she called to her dogs, who kept stopping to sniff under practically every bush along the side of the trail. "We're late for dinner!"

Artemis picked up her pace. With her dogs trotting along at her heels, she reached the Academy in less than twenty minutes. (And luckily didn't get lost once!) After crossing the courtyard and climbing the granite steps to the bronze front doors, they headed inside to the school's cafeteria.

# 5
# More Boy Trouble

"HI! YOU'RE LATE," APHRODITE COMMENTED when Artemis plonked her dinner tray down at the table she and her three BFFs always shared. Stunningly beautiful, Aphrodite had golden hair that was threaded with sparkly pink ribbons. As befitted the goddessgirl of love and beauty, the ruffled rose-pink chiton she wore looked fantastic on her. Artemis

guessed it must be the newest style, though she couldn't say for sure. Fashion had never been her thing, even though she admired the clothing choices of others.

"Yeah, I know," Artemis replied. Not even bothering to slip her bow and quiver of arrows from her back as she sat down, she nodded in greeting to Persephone and Athena, who were also at the table. Amby, Nectar, and Suez took their usual spots underneath and near her feet. It was a good place to wait for treats.

Sure enough, they were rewarded seconds later when Artemis pulled apart a bread roll and tossed pieces of it onto the floor. They jostled to gobble them.

Aphrodite raised a perfectly shaped eyebrow. "You're hardly ever late for a meal," she said to Artemis. "Something happen?"

She nodded. "I was out walking my dogs on the

trail along the river," she started to explain. "But then I got this strange feeling that something wasn't quite right, and—"

"And you discovered you'd made a wrong turn and gotten lost?" Persephone interrupted before Artemis could go on. Giving her a fond look, Persephone twirled a lock of her long curly red hair around one finger. A beautiful yellow rose was tucked behind one of her ears. She was the goddess-girl of spring and growing plants, and often wore flowers in her hair.

Before replying, Artemis opened her carton of nectar and took a sip. Nectar helped keep the goddesses and gods youthful and immortal. It also caused their skin to shimmer as if lightly powdered by glitter. She swallowed, and then answered matter-of-factly. "No, the wrong turn happened later."

Her friends laughed. Apollo wasn't the only one who was aware of her poor sense of direction and liked to tease her about it!

Her BFFs had already finished eating, she noticed. And they'd stacked their plates onto a single tray, ready to take back to the tray return. They probably would've left the cafeteria by now but had waited around just for her. It was one of many small examples of why they were the best buds ever!

"Okay, so tell us the real reason you're late," Athena prodded. Brown-haired, with striking gray-blue eyes, Zeus's brainy daughter was the goddessgirl of wisdom, among other things.

Artemis hungrily forked up a bite of nectaroni and cheese. As she ate, she told her friends what had happened while she was out walking her dogs. They all knew about her twin sense, and that she shared

a lesser but similar bond with the nymphs. So she didn't have to explain why she'd been able to sense that someone needed her help. When she told them how Alpheus had tricked Arethusa into promising to go out with him, they all frowned in disapproval.

"That is *so* not cool," said Athena. The others nodded in agreement.

"Yeah," said Artemis. "So, after talking with the nymphs, I paid Alpheus a visit," she went on. "I tried to get him to release Arethusa from her promise and asked him to give me the cup he took from her when she drank from his river. I said I would return it to her. He wouldn't do it, though. Not yet, anyway. He said he'd think about it, and told me to come back tomorrow morning."

By the time she finished her story, her BFFs were frowning even harder. "That river rat!" Persephone

said. "He should've given you Arethusa's cup right away!"

"And tricking a girl is certainly *not* the way to get her to like you!" exclaimed Aphrodite. She ought to know. Tons of boys, both mortal and immortal, were always trying to get this beautiful goddessgirl's attention.

"That's for sure," Athena said in agreement. She looked at Artemis. "He sounds despicable. But you said he was kind to your dogs, right? And that you actually enjoyed talking to him?"

Artemis nodded as she fed more scraps to Amby, Suez, and Nectar.

"Hmm," said Aphrodite. She tapped her chin with a sparkly pink-polished fingertip, a sure sign she was thinking. At last she said, "Sounds like he's not *all* bad. I wonder why he thinks he needs to

trick a girl into promising to go out with him. Seems oddly desperate."

Artemis shrugged. "Who knows? Aside from stealing the cup and demanding that promise, he was . . . *likable*. And friendly. It was weird. Question is, how can I get him to release Arethusa from that promise and give me her cup when I see him tomorrow?" She glanced around the table at her friends. "Ideas, anyone?"

Athena's forehead wrinkled in thought. After a moment, she said, "Maybe *you* could offer something in trade?"

Artemis dipped a spoon into a small bowl of delicious ambrosia pudding. "I thought about that. But what? Arethusa already tried offering other stuff in trade. Maybe her offers just weren't anything he needed?"

"Well, he doesn't exactly *need* to go out with Arethusa, either," scoffed Aphrodite.

The girls all went silent for a while, thinking.

Persephone was the first to pipe up with an idea. "Think Alpheus might be interested in a tour of the Underworld? As a trade, I mean? I'd have to get Hades's permission before you could ask Alpheus, though."

Hades was godboy of the Underworld, where mortals went after they died. There they became *shades*, another name for human souls. Since he was Persephone's crush, she could probably convince him to let Alpheus visit. But though Persephone had grown fond of the gloomy place, Artemis couldn't imagine anyone else voluntarily wanting to tour it. She refrained from saying so, though, not wanting to hurt Persephone's feelings.

"Or how about a ride in my swan cart?" suggested Aphrodite. The small ceramic double-swan cart she kept on a knickknack shelf in her room was magical. Whenever she chanted it to life, it would grow so big that its orange-beaked swans' wings stretched six feet across and its golden cart could fit several people at once.

"I'm not sure if he ever leaves his river," Artemis said to both girls. "But I could ask."

"I could plant olive trees along his riverbank," Athena offered.

Artemis remembered the silvery willows that bordered it and doubted that Alpheus would care about adding more trees, but she just nodded. "I'll ask him," she said as she scraped up the last of her pudding. "Thanks for all the thoughts, you guys."

Suddenly Athena jumped up from the table. "Ye

gods! I almost forgot! I'm supposed to meet Heracles at the library in a few minutes to study for a Science-ology test."

Artemis scrunched her nose. "But it's the weekend! When's the test?" Science-ology wasn't one of her classes.

"Next Friday," Athena admitted a bit sheepishly.

The other girls laughed.

"So it's a week away? Kind of last-minute prep for you, isn't it?" Persephone teased lightly. The brainy Athena always over-prepared and would never cram for an exam the night before, the way lots of students did.

Aphrodite grinned. "I bet Heracles only agreed to the study session because it gives him a chance to be with you."

Athena took the teasing good-naturedly. "Maybe,"

she said in response to both comments. She reached for the tray piled with dishes in the center of the table.

Aphrodite waved her off. "We'll take care of that. You go on."

"Thanks," said Athena. She smiled at her friends. "See you all later!" Watching her rush from the cafeteria, Artemis glanced around for Actaeon. She hadn't seen him when she'd first come in, but she'd been late, of course. By now the cafeteria was nearly empty, and he obviously wasn't here.

"I'd better get going, too," Aphrodite said now. "Ares invited me to meet him and a bunch of others to play Episkyros tonight. But I need to change into a sportier outfit first."

Episkyros was a ball game played between two teams of a dozen to fourteen members each. A white

line called the *skuros* ran between the teams, and there was also a line behind each team. Each team would try to throw the ball over the heads of the other team until one team was finally forced behind its own line.

"So what are *your* plans?" Aphrodite asked Artemis and Persephone as the three girls rose from the table. Seeing them get up, Artemis's dogs scrambled to their feet. They trotted along behind Artemis and her friends as the girls carried the empty dishes to the tray return.

"I was supposed to meet Actaeon here in the cafeteria after dinner," Artemis replied. "We were going to go to the Supernatural Market for shakes."

Persephone glanced around. "Hmm. I saw him in here earlier, but it looks like he's gone."

"Maybe he went on to the market without me."

Artemis tried not to feel hurt that he hadn't waited for her like her friends had.

"Hades and I are going there too," Persephone told her. "He's meeting me outside in the courtyard in a few. Want to come with? If Actaeon isn't there, you can still hang out with us and have a nice tasty shake."

Artemis brightened. "That sounds great. I just need to take my dogs up to my room first." By the time she ran them upstairs and came back down, Hades had joined Persephone in the courtyard.

The Supernatural Market was basically a snack shop with some tables at the back, located just beyond the edge of campus. As the three of them headed there, Artemis saw that Hades and Persephone were holding hands. They made an adorable couple. She wondered if anyone thought that about her and Actaeon when they saw them together.

When they arrived at the market, Artemis heard a familiar laugh coming from the back of the market. Her heart lifted. Actaeon was here! At the same time she again felt a twinge of annoyance. Why hadn't he waited for her at MOA? She would've waited for him if he'd been late!

Hades and Persephone paused just inside the snack shop's entrance to look at the latest issue of *Teen Scrollazine* on a rack at the front of the shop. It was a great source of news and gossip about all the goddesses and gods, and Artemis couldn't help glancing at the newest headlines. The lead article was about a trivia game that had taken Mount Olympus by storm recently when a girl named Hecate, who now attended MOA part-time, had visited the Academy.

Artemis was eager to see Actaeon, and so eased past the scrollazine rack and several shelves of

snacks to the back of the shop. *There he is!* She spotted her crush sitting at one of the round tables next to a pretty mortal girl. There were two empty shake glasses on their table, she noticed at once. Had they sat there together and drunk them?

The girl was leaning toward Actaeon, whose back was to Artemis, as he showed her a magic trick involving two drinking straws. First holding them to form a big plus sign, he wrapped one around the other to make what appeared to be a large knot at the center. Then he folded the top and bottom halves of the vertical straw so that both straws were now nestled together horizontally, still linked in the middle by the knot.

"Now watch carefully," he said to the girl. He blew on the knot. "Presto change-o. Straws unlink-o!" He pulled on the ends of the straws. Immediately they came apart, both of them straight and whole.

Artemis's stomach knotted as the girl giggled and clapped. Who was she, anyway? The straw trick was one Artemis had seen Actaeon do before. For *her*. Until now, she'd thought she was the only girl he'd ever performed it for!

The girl touched Actaeon's arm. "You're so clever. Show it to me again, okay?"

Was she *flirting* with him? Artemis stepped up to the table. "It's just an illusion," she announced. "Since Actaeon's a mortal, he can't do *real* magic."

The girl drew back at her snarky tone, but Actaeon didn't seem to notice her annoyance. Either that or he was ignoring it.

Smiling, he leaped to his feet. "Artemis! Hey! I was beginning to think you weren't coming. Glad you made it. Want a shake?"

"No thanks," Artemis said flatly. Until now, she'd

never understood how some girls could become jealous over a boy, but suddenly she found herself in exactly that position. Giving the pretty girl a sidelong glance, she added, "Looks to me like you've already *got* company."

"Huh?" The look on Actaeon's face changed to one of confusion. "Excuse us," he said to the girl. He went over to Artemis and touched her arm. "Hey, let's go outside and talk," he suggested quietly.

*Uh-oh,* thought Artemis. Her jealous feelings drained away as readily as they had come. Fear spiked in her heart. Was it possible that her crush was about to tell her he'd decided to become her ex-crush?

# 6
# A Misunderstanding

"I LOOKED FOR YOU AT DINNER," ACTAEON SAID to Artemis as they stepped outside the Supernatural Market. "But you never showed."

They automatically began to walk back toward the MOA campus and sports fields. Artemis was so nervous that she quickened her pace as they walked, and Actaeon had to practically jog to keep up with

her. It was like she was trying to run away from what he might say!

"Yeah, sorry I was late," she mumbled. "But I figured you'd wait for me."

"I did," Actaeon told her, jogging ever faster to keep up. "For a while, anyway." His hand brushed the back of hers as they walk-jogged, but he didn't try to link his fingers with hers. She almost reached for his hand, but then held back. She wanted to hear what he would say first. Especially if he was going to crush her feelings by un-crushing on her. As in break up with her!

Actaeon went on. "When you didn't show up, I started to think I'd remembered wrong. That maybe we'd agreed to meet at the Supernatural Market instead of the cafeteria. So I headed there."

Artemis nodded. If things had been reversed and

it was Actaeon who'd been late, she might have wondered that too, and then done the same thing. She decided to change the subject. "So did you guys have fun at Game On!?" she asked, slowing down a little.

For a fraction of a second an unhappy shadow passed over Actaeon's face. But then it was gone, and he simply shrugged. "It was okay." As they came even with the archery field behind the gym, he suddenly suggested, "Hey, how about some target practice before we go back?"

"Sure," said Artemis. He wanted to spend more time with her. *Woo-hoo!* Feeling more lighthearted, she grinned at him. "But I'm warning you. I've trained my silver arrows a lot over the past week. There's no chance I'll miss the bull's-eye. Even from two hundred feet out!"

Actaeon grinned back. "Bring it on! I've been

training my arrows too. So far they know how to *sit*, *stay*, and *heel*. We're still working on *hit the center of the bull's-eye*, though."

Artemis laughed. Of course he was joking. Actaeon was an excellent archer. Still, the fact that he was mortal meant he didn't have magical arrows he could instruct like she did. And that would always make for unequal contests between them.

Magical arrows were worthless without good training, however. Artemis spent countless hours every week teaching hers how best to navigate distance and wind currents to reach their intended targets.

As if Actaeon had read her thoughts, he said, "It's true that your arrows' magic does give you an advantage we mere mortals don't enjoy." He said this lightly, but she thought she detected a slight

edge to his voice. Which was strange. Because he'd never seemed to mind before that she, being immortal, could utilize magic. While he, being mortal, could not.

But then Actaeon sent her a sweet look and changed the subject. "So, are you going to tell me why you were so late getting back to MOA tonight?" he asked as they walked onto the archery field. "You didn't get lost, did you?" he teased.

So he knew about her lousy sense of direction? She didn't recall ever admitting it to him. *Humph*—no doubt Apollo had mentioned it.

Artemis gave Actaeon's arm a playful shove. "Nuh-uh. I didn't. Well, not for long, anyway."

He chuckled, then went to fetch the bow and arrows he'd left in the sports equipment shed at the edge of the archery field earlier that day. After

he got them, Artemis explained about meeting the nymphs on the trail, coaxing Arethusa up from the bottom of the well to talk, and her conversation with the river god Alpheus.

Actaeon listened as they took turns shooting at one of the many round targets set up at the far end of the field. When she'd finished talking, he frowned. "That river god sounds very uncool. I can't believe he didn't return your nymph friend's cup. What he did is just not right."

"True," Artemis agreed. "Only he is a god, and—"

"And immortals can do as they like to lesser beings, including nymphs . . . and mortals like me," Actaeon finished for her. His cheeks flamed red with anger.

Artemis blinked at him in surprise. What was going on here? Actaeon was always so easygoing.

She'd never seen him get mad like this. Had it begun to bother him that he was mortal while she was a goddess? Why, though, when it hadn't seemed to matter in the past? She opened her mouth to ask, but then closed it. Because what if the answer was something she'd rather not hear?

So far they'd both been hitting bull's-eyes with their arrows. To make things more challenging, they increased their distance from the targets and chose some that could magically dodge arrows! It was a school rule that *all* arrows in use at MOA had to be dipped in the Pool of Magic in the Forest of the Beasts in order to render them safe. That way neither magical nor non-magical arrows could actually wound anyone by accident, no matter how daring the competition became.

Actaeon grimaced when his next two arrows

missed the bull's-eye to stick in the lower ring. "And another thing," he went on as he watched her step up to their new shooting line. "This river god sounds like the sneaky sort. Maybe you should avoid him. I don't see why you're getting in the middle of this. It seems to me that things typically only get worse for most mortals and lesser beings when gods and goddesses interfere."

*Godzooks!* thought Artemis as she fitted the notched end of an arrow into her bow. He sounded way bitter about that! Was he recalling the time she'd gotten angry at him and used her magic to change him into a stag? After that, her dogs and a deer-hunting giant had chased after him. Later, he'd called it an "interesting experience," but maybe that wasn't how he'd really felt. Did he actually resent it? It had to have been a little frightening.

"Arethusa *asked* for my help," she informed him as she pulled her bowstring taut and sighted along her arrow. Speaking more sharply than she meant to, she added, "I'd be shirking my duty as her protector if I didn't 'interfere,' as you call it."

She released her arrow. *Zzzing!* It knocked both of Actaeon's arrows off the lower ring of the target before hitting the middle of the bull's-eye, its tip sticking right beside her other two arrows.

Actaeon grimaced again as his arrows fell to the ground. Gamely, however, he drew another arrow from his quiver. "Don't you think it's possible that your friend and the other nymphs might be better off if you let them solve their own problems? At least sometimes?" he asked as he nocked the arrow and pulled his bowstring tight.

With a start, Artemis remembered how, back at

the well, she'd actually thought that very thing. No way was she going to admit that to Actaeon, however. Because he was being kind of annoying!

Actaeon released his arrow. *Zzzing!* After a wobbly flight, it fell to the ground to land beside his other two arrows. He stared at them in frustrated dismay. "I just can't seem to do anything right today," he muttered.

Artemis's irritation toward him evaporated instantly. She knew what it was like to have a bad day, after all. Didn't everyone? "Well, I could use magic on the target to make it easier for you to hit, if that'll help," she teased gently.

Normally, Actaeon would have cracked a smile at this, or laughed. But not today. After casting a hurt look her way, he hurried over and grabbed his arrows. Silently, and without stopping to return his

equipment to the storage shed, he stalked off the field toward the Academy.

Stunned, Artemis froze for a few seconds. But then she rushed after him. "Hey, wait. It was just a joke. I was trying to cheer you up!"

"Really? Well, you failed," Actaeon called over his shoulder. "I hope you do better for Arethusa tomorrow."

Huh? His retort couldn't have stung her more than if he'd hit her with one of his arrows. (One that had found its mark, that is!)

She halted in her tracks. "Fine!" she yelled after him. "Be that way!"

Retracing her steps, she stomped back to the edge of the archery field. "Come, Opsis, Loxos, and Hekaergos!" she called to her three silver arrows. Magically, they plucked themselves from the

bull's-eye at the center of the target and flew back to her in a flash.

After stowing them in her quiver, she headed for the Academy too. She hoped Actaeon would calm down by the time she arrived and be waiting for her just inside the big bronze doors. But he was nowhere in sight when she entered. With a heavy heart, and an unhappy lump in her throat, Artemis climbed the staircase to the girls' dorm.

# 7

# Something to Trade

WHEN ARTEMIS OPENED THE DOOR TO HER room, her dogs practically bowled her over. "Hey, nice to know *you guys* are glad to see me, at least." She squatted on the floor and gave them a group hug, running her hands over their soft fur. Despite this, a few tears leaked from her eyes. As they rolled down her cheeks, Suez licked them away. Being with animals always had

a soothing effect on Artemis. After a bit, her heart calmed and the lump in her throat shrank.

It was only as she was getting ready for bed a short time later that Artemis wondered if she should've sent a notescroll to Arethusa. A message to let her know what Alpheus had said during their talk that afternoon. It wasn't too late to summon a magic breeze to whoosh that information to the nymph. Magic breezes delivered all kinds of messages around Mount Olympus and beyond.

However, telling Arethusa that she hadn't been able to get the river god to return the cup or release her from her promise—not yet, anyway—might not be the best plan. It might only upset her and even cause her to spend a sleepless night hiding at the bottom of that damp well. There was no real need to

tell her how things stood now. Better to say nothing than to tell her bad news, right?

Instead, she'd drop by tomorrow morning to let Arethusa know what was going on, Artemis decided. Then, she'd head to the river to bargain with Alpheus. Once he'd officially agreed to release Arethusa from her promise, Artemis would have *good* news to share.

Although she hoped Arethusa would sleep peacefully tonight, sleep proved hard for Artemis herself. She kept considering different ways the conversation with Alpheus might go the next morning, trying to get it all straight in her head. Surely she'd be able to persuade him to make some kind of trade.

She tossed and turned, making her crumpled, slightly dog-scented sheets even more tangled than they normally were. *Hmm.* Maybe it really *was* about

time to wash them, along with the virtual mountain range of clothes on her floor. It was a good thing boys weren't allowed in the girls' dorm rooms, because she'd be majorly embarrassed if Actaeon ever saw her room like this!

She thought now of his reaction to her handling of Arethusa's request for help. What he'd said about immortals doing whatever they liked to beings such as nymphs and mortals had really hurt. And it wasn't true! Not exactly, anyway. Yes, the goddesses and gods did intervene in other beings' fortunes, but it was usually because those beings *asked* them to. Were she and other immortals just supposed to ignore such requests?

And while the magical powers immortals possessed could put "lesser" beings (*his* term, not hers) at a disadvantage, those same magical powers were

often used to help them! Sometimes immortals made things worse, it was true. But rarely on purpose. She certainly couldn't recall ever having done so herself.

The more Artemis thought about all this, the more irked at Actaeon she became. In her opinion he'd acted quite unreasonably. She mulled over the things he'd said on the archery field earlier that evening. All at once she remembered the words he'd muttered after missing the target for the third time during their last game: "I just can't seem to do anything right today."

Now it occurred to her to wonder what else had gone wrong for him today. Why hadn't she asked? Instead, she'd made that dumb joke about using magic to make it easier for him to hit the target. *Argh!* It just went to show—again—how bad she was at crush stuff.

If only she'd asked, maybe Actaeon wouldn't have stalked off. Things might have ended very differently—like with them strolling hand in hand into the Academy together!

It was after midnight before Artemis finally fell asleep, exhausted by imagining what she could have said or done to avert a crush-aster. Toward morning she dreamed that she was out walking along the same trail as yesterday, only without her dogs this time. Nearing Alpheus's river, she took a wrong step and fell off the bank into a fast-flowing part of the river.

"Help!" she cried out as she was swept downstream. Though she thrashed about in the water, she was unable to gain control and climb out. As she sank deeper, water flowed over her head, and—just then, she woke up. Nectar was standing on top of her, licking her face.

"Hey, thanks," Artemis told him, gently lifting his paws from her chest and rolling out from under him. "Do you offer towels with your drooly showers?" Nectar just wagged his tail and jumped down from the bed.

Her dream faded rapidly as she went to her room's only window, which looked out on the Academy courtyard. Squinting, she read the sundial that stood down there. *Ye gods!* It was after eight already. That would normally be early for a Saturday morning, but she needed to get a move on if she was going to visit Arethusa before meeting up with Alpheus at nine.

She would take her chariot, she decided. That would get her to the trail much faster than walking.

She dashed down the hall for a quick shower. Then, back in her room, she rummaged through

her mountains of laundry, searching for a clean (or at least almost-clean) chiton.

Super-neat Aphrodite was always urging her to hang things up. But what was the point of that? She'd be trading the time it took to go through the piles on her floor with the time it took to riffle through her closet. Same difference, right? And, speaking of time, it seemed to her that tossing a piece of clothing onto a pile was much faster than hanging it up, faster even than casting a magic spell to do the task. So her method actually *saved* time!

"Aha!" She'd spotted the hem of her favorite red chiton sticking out from under a bunch of wrinkled socks and tights. She pulled it from the pile and sniffed it. "Fresh enough," she concluded. And there was only a small stain on the back of it. Hardly even noticeable.

Pulling it closer, she saw that the stain was actually a paw print. Likely Amby's, from the size of it. Artemis slipped the chiton over her head and smoothed out the wrinkles as best she could. Definitely time to do laundry. One of these days. When she had time. Maybe.

Her dogs stretched, and then wandered around the room while she refilled their food and water bowls. "Here's the plan, boys," she told them after she'd finished her task and they were eating and drinking. "I'm not going to take you with me when I go see the nymphs and Alpheus this morning. Sorry about that, but we'll go for a short walk now and a longer one later, okay?"

*Ruff!* barked Suez, as if he understood and accepted the situation even though he might not like it. He ran over and pawed at her door. Amby and

Nectar joined him, and the dogs spilled out into the hallway once she opened it.

After taking them for a brisk walk around the edge of the courtyard, Artemis brought them back to her room. As she was about to head downstairs to the cafeteria, she glanced at the knickknack shelf above her bed and noticed the small gold figure of her three dogs frolicking with a little gold ball. Hephaestus, the godboy of metalworking, had made it for her. The gift had been meant for her temple in Ephesus, but she'd decided to keep it in her room since she liked it so much.

If all else failed, maybe she could get Alpheus to take it in trade for releasing Arethusa from her promise? Before she could think too hard about how reluctant she'd be to give it up, she dropped the figure into her quiver. After slipping her bow

and quiver of arrows across her back, she said bye to her dogs and left her room.

Her friends were already at their usual table when she entered the cafeteria. She hurried over to them. "Hey," she said breathlessly when they looked up and saw her. "I'm just here to grab some snacks before I take my chariot to the river. I overslept and don't have time for breakfast, so I'll just see you guys when I get back."

"Wait!" Aphrodite cocked her head. "I'm thinking maybe we should go with you."

"Yeah," said Athena. "We might be able to help you convince Alpheus to drop the promise Arethusa made."

After swallowing a bite of hambrosia, Persephone nodded. "Or at least we can offer you moral support."

Briefly Artemis considered the idea, but then she

shook her head. "Thanks, but I'll go by myself. If we all go, Alpheus might feel like we're ganging up on him. Which might make him dig in his heels and refuse to back down even more."

"You have a point, I guess," Aphrodite said reluctantly. She picked up an apple from her tray and took a bite.

"If you change your mind, though, just send us a message by magic breeze," Athena added.

Persephone put down her fork. "Yeah, we can hop in Aphrodite's swan cart and be at the river in minutes if you need us."

After her BFFs wished her good luck, Artemis grabbed a bread roll, a hunk of cheese, and an orange from the snack table to scarf down on her trip. Before heading out of the cafeteria, she saw Actaeon enter. When he glanced her way, she ducked

her head and pretended not to see him. She hadn't really meant to do that, but once she had, there was no taking it back. She just hoped he hadn't noticed it and thought she was being mean or something.

He'd made it clear last night that he didn't think it was a good idea for her to "interfere" in Arethusa's boy trouble. So he'd certainly disapprove of what she was about to do, and she didn't want him to try to talk her out of it. Though the nymphs would view her meeting with Alpheus as heroic, Actaeon wouldn't see it that way at all. Anyway, she didn't have time to talk to him right now.

When she finally dared to peek again, she saw that Actaeon was standing at the food counter with his back to her. He and some friends were waiting for Ms. Okto, the school's eight-armed lunch lady, to hand over plates of hambrosia and scrambled eggs.

Artemis stuffed her snacks into her quiver. *Hmm.* After lugging this food around, she should probably add cleaning the inside of her quiver to her list of projects. No time to think about that now, though! She hurried out of the cafeteria to the Academy's entrance, and then raced outside down the granite steps to the marble-tiled courtyard.

MOA had chariots that students could use with Zeus's permission. But Artemis kept her own chariot on the school grounds. Zeus had made an exception for it after four milk-white deer with golden horns had followed her back from a second-grade field trip to Mount Parnassus in southern Greece. Those deer became her pets, and they enjoyed nothing more than pulling her chariot.

Because the chariot was magical, they were able to harness themselves to it at a moment's notice. Now,

at her whistled summons, the four deer appeared in the courtyard, pulling her chariot behind them. She jumped in and took up the reins. Magic chants often worked best when they rhymed, so she gave it a shot even though she was kind of tired this morning.

*"Chariot, take me to Arethusa.*

*Hurry, there's no time to lose-uh!"*

As rhyming commands went, it wasn't the best. Luckily, her deer understood and obeyed.

They lifted off at once. As the chariot zoomed upward, the sun glinted off the polished white stone of the majestic five-story Academy. Surrounded on all sides by dozens of Ionic columns, it also had low-relief friezes sculpted just below its peaked rooftop. It was mega-amazing!

The milk-white deer sailed her chariot over the top of the olive grove that grew to one side of the

courtyard, then quickly whooshed her down to the forest. The minute they landed, the deer magically unhitched themselves from the chariot and leaped away to graze along the trail. No sooner had Artemis stepped onto the ground than Arethusa appeared. And seconds later, her four tree-nymph friends swung down from their trees as well.

# 8 Complications

SMILING BIG, ARETHUSA RAN UP AND HUGGED Artemis. "I knew you'd come! You're here to tell me you got Alpheus to release me from my promise, right?"

"Um . . . well . . . uh," began Artemis.

"Of course that's why Artemis is here," said Pitys, the pine-tree-loving nymph. "She'd never let us down!"

Flipping her long sea-green hair over one shoulder, Arethusa went on gushing to Artemis. "You're the best! The most fantastic goddessgirl of them all."

"For sure!" echoed Dicte. That was high praise, considering how negative this nymph could sometimes be, but Artemis wasn't sure she deserved it. At all. And now she really, *really* didn't want to admit that she hadn't gotten Alpheus to release Arethusa from her promise!

Syke grabbed Arethusa around the waist and twirled with her in a circle. "Didn't I say we could depend on Artemis!" she crowed.

Giggling, Karya squinched up her nose and made a funny face. "Yeah! It would be *nutty* not to!" She was cradling a cute little brown-and-white puppy in her arms, Artemis noticed now. *Hello? When and where did she get that little guy?* she wondered.

Before she could ask, Karya buried her face in the puppy's soft fur and murmured, "Alpheus should look for a girl who really likes him."

"Yeah, no kidding!" said Arethusa as she executed another twirl on her own. "Which means he might have to look far and wide!"

All the nymphs except Karya giggled at this. She smiled goofily. "Maybe, maybe not. You never know. I bet lots of girls like him."

"Ha! That meanie? Not a chance!" Dicte scoffed.

Arethusa stopped twirling and looked at Artemis. "Do tell us how you did it," she begged. "We can't wait to hear the story!" She glanced toward the chariot. "Is my cup in there?" she asked, since she could see for herself that Artemis wasn't holding it. "Or maybe in your quiver?"

Artemis gulped. She hoped Arethusa and the

others wouldn't be too upset when they learned the truth. "Here's the thing," she began. "Alpheus has proven to be more of a challenge than I thought he would be."

"Oh no! You mean you *don't* have my cup?" Arethusa asked, sounding confused.

"Well, not yet," Artemis admitted reluctantly.

A look of panic came into the nymph's eyes. "But that cup is *special*. I must get it back!" she practically shrieked.

"Yes, yes, I know," Artemis said, wincing at the girl's obvious alarm. "Dicte told me your dad carved it and gave it to you when you were a baby. So I understand why—"

"That's true," Arethusa interrupted her to say. "But that's not the only reason it's special. You see, it has certain . . . um . . . *powers*."

"You mean it really *is* magical?" Artemis asked in surprise.

"Huh?" said Arethusa. "How did you—" Breaking off speaking, she narrowed accusing eyes at Karya.

The girl's face went a little pink. "Whoops-a-daisy," she said. There was regret in her eyes as she met Arethusa's gaze. "Sorry I told your secret. It just sort of popped out of my mouth without my permission."

Arethusa sighed. "It's okay," she told Karya. "I know how hard it is for you to keep secrets. When I told you about my cup, the words just sort of slipped out of my mouth without my permission too!"

She looked back at Artemis. "I'm sorry I didn't tell you. See, my dad put some magic into the cup when he carved it. He said it would protect me from harm while I was growing up. But he also warned me to keep the cup a secret." She paused, frowning.

"Why?" Syke asked. "Was he worried that if anyone knew about its protective powers, they might try to steal it, hoping it would offer *them* protection?"

Arethusa shook her head. "Not exactly. It was because the cup's magic can increase the magic powers of whoever possesses it. Kind of an unintentional side effect of the protection spell, my dad said. But it's one effect that can't be removed. So if it ever falls into the wrong immortal's hands, which I guess it has . . ."

"Such a cup could bring disaster!" Artemis finished. "Even if Alpheus doesn't mean any harm, suddenly gaining amazing newfound abilities might cause him to become a bit power-hungry and bring about harm anyway. Anyone might do the same, whether purposely or by accident!"

Arethusa blushed. "Well, yeah."

It flashed on Artemis then that Arethusa might

not have told her this till now because Artemis herself was an immortal. It kind of hurt to think that the nymph might suspect Artemis of trying to steal the cup to increase her own powers. After all, they were friends! Even if Artemis had known the cup was magical, she would *never, ever* have done such a thing. Didn't Arethusa know that?

Suddenly, Actaeon's words came back to her again: ". . . and immortals can do as they like to lesser beings, including nymphs and mortals like me."

Was this what Arethusa thought too? Well, that stung!

"Think Alpheus knows the cup has magic?" asked Karya, clutching the puppy close with a worried look on her sweet face.

"Probably not, or he'd have already refused to ever give it up," Artemis assured her.

But although she didn't think the river god was evil, and did think he was kind of funny at times, he was also sneaky and self-centered. Which meant this cup situation had just become more urgent. She needed to get it back from him before he realized its power!

"So does this mean Alpheus still expects me to go out with him?" Arethusa blurted out, her voice rising in dismay.

"Yes, but I'm meeting with him again after I leave here, so you shouldn't—" Before she could finish saying that Arethusa shouldn't give up hope, the nymph fainted!

Syke caught her before she could fall to the ground. While she cradled the girl, Dicte frowned at Artemis. "Look what you've done! You're supposed to be our protector. It's part of your goddess

job!" she cried out. Her normally pale cheeks were flushed with anger.

The other nymphs, who had gathered around Arethusa to fan her face with leaves, began frowning at Artemis too.

"I know that," Artemis said a bit testily. "I'm doing my best."

Did Dicte truly believe that she wasn't taking her duty seriously? All the goddesses and gods of Mount Olympus were mega-serious about their obligations to others. If they ever weren't, Zeus would call them on it. She shivered, not wanting to think about what that thunderbolt-happy, superstrong King of the Gods might do if he thought she wasn't capable of doing her job.

Still, couldn't these nymphs just be grateful that Artemis had tried at all? And was going to try again?

Apparently not. Instead, they didn't completely trust her and maybe even suspected that she might steal a magic cup, given half a chance.

Briefly she wondered if Actaeon had been right to doubt the wisdom of her being drawn into the middle of Arethusa's boy trouble. She even opened her mouth to suggest to Dicte that if she didn't think Artemis could help, maybe she should go talk to Alpheus herself. Before she could utter the words, however, Arethusa recovered.

"Ooh, sorry. I fainted, huh?" She gave Artemis a shaky smile. "I'm not really mad at you, and I do trust you with my cup. I know you're trying to help. Alpheus is stubborn, though. Tricky, too. Lucky for me, you're much cleverer than he is. So I know you'll get him to change his mind about that stupid promise. And, most importantly, you'll rescue my cup!"

"Of course she will," Pitys assured the girl.

"No question!" Syke agreed, patting Arethusa's shoulder.

*Nothing like putting on the pressure,* Artemis thought to herself. However, it was nice that they seemed to still trust her.

Karya looked up from petting the puppy. "It would be nuts to think she wouldn't." She frowned at Dicte. "Right?"

For a moment Dicte said nothing. But then she nodded her head. "Right."

Not wanting to dwell on how disappointed these nymphs must be with her, Artemis went over and gave the puppy Karya held a pat. It squirmed happily. "He's so cute," she couldn't resist saying. "How long have you had him? Is he new?"

"He's a stray," Karya told her. "I found him

wandering around in our forest. I think someone just left him here, poor thing." She hugged the little dog and cooed, "I'm going to take good care of you from now on, though, you sweet baby-waby."

"Lucky dog. Lucky that you found him, I mean," said Artemis, stroking its smooth, glossy fur. "Does he have a name?"

"Chester," Karya replied quickly. "Because sweet chestnuts are one of my favorite nuts."

Artemis nodded, grinning in spite of her current troubles. "Chester," she repeated. "A cute name for a cute puppy. I like it!"

Shading her eyes, she glanced upward, noticing the position of Helios's sun chariot overhead. "Gotta go!" she said to the nymphs hurriedly. "I told Alpheus I'd meet him at nine and I'm running a bit late."

Putting two fingers between her lips, she whistled for her deer. Immediately, they stopped grazing and leaped over to her chariot. Within seconds, they'd hitched themselves to it again. The nymphs watched as Artemis climbed inside and took up the reins. "I'll return later. With your cup!" she promised Arethusa with more confidence than she actually felt.

"To the river!" she called. Her deer sprang away to do as she commanded. The nymphs all waved as her chariot took to the sky. Their expressions ranged from worried to hopeful. With renewed determination, Artemis waved back.

All too soon, her chariot set down alongside the river in the same place she had met Alpheus the day before. He rose from the water almost instantly and waded to shore as she jumped to the ground. "Good to see ya again!" he greeted her cheerily. He spun

himself around and around like a mini tornado, slicking off water droplets. By the time he halted, he was completely dry. "I was beginning to worry you wouldn't show."

This made Artemis think of Actaeon's comment from the night before. About how when she hadn't appeared in the cafeteria at dinner, he'd started to worry that he'd remembered wrong. And how when she hadn't shown, he'd gone to the Supernatural Market without her. Where he'd decided to hang out with that unknown girl. *Ugh.* Feeling a jolt of sadness, she tried to shake off the memory.

Before she could dwell on it further, Alpheus interrupted her thoughts. "But it's good to see that—unlike a certain nymph we both know whose name starts and ends with *A*—you're someone who keeps her promises," he added slyly.

Artemis gave a snort of laughter. He was correct about her keeping her promises, or trying to, anyway. She got right to the point. "I've come prepared to make a trade," she announced firmly. "One that'll have you agreeing to return Arethusa's cup and forgetting about her promise to you."

Instead of responding to her superconfident assertion immediately, he calmly went over to her deer. They'd unhitched themselves from the chariot but were still standing near it. "You must be thirsty, guys. Please drink from my river," he said to them as he reached to stroke the nearest one's back.

He glanced up at Artemis and, as if he'd read her mind, added, "No strings attached. I promise."

Artemis nodded to her deer, which had turned their heads to look at her in question. "It's okay," she told them gently. "Go ahead and drink."

"Do they have names?" Alpheus asked as the deer wandered down to the edge of the river and began to lap up some cool, sweet water. He sat down in a grassy spot nearby, waving Artemis over to sit too. Sunshine glinted on the silver streaks in his bright blue hair.

Though she didn't want to stay any longer than she had to, Artemis sat. She shrugged off her bow and quiver of arrows and set them on the ground between Alpheus and herself. Pointing to each of her deer in turn, she named them. "The smallest one is Delta. The others are Hypatia, Eudora, and Callista."

Alpheus smiled at her. "Nice. I've heard that you love animals. So do I." Sounding almost shy, he added, "I bet we have a lotta other things in common too."

*Ye gods!* she thought. Was he . . . flirting with her? But no, that couldn't be. Not if he was so in like with Arethusa that he'd tricked her into promising to go out with him! Too bad Aphrodite wasn't here. She'd be able to judge, but Artemis wasn't good at that kind of thing.

"Doubt it," Artemis replied briskly, hoping to put a stop to things if this godboy really was becoming interested in her. "So, anyway, did you bring Arethusa's cup with you?"

Alpheus nodded.

"Then where is it?" Artemis asked, since she could see he didn't have it.

Playfully, Alpheus wagged a finger at her. "Not so fast. It's somewhere safe, close by." Becoming more serious, he cocked his head. "You mentioned a possible trade?"

Artemis nodded. Then, as her deer sauntered over to nibble on some bushes near the river's edge, she described the offers her goddessgirl friends had come up with yesterday in the cafeteria.

"Big no to the Underworld tour," Alpheus said, after she'd finished listing them. He wrinkled his nose. "Too stinky down there, or so I've heard."

"Then how about the swan-cart ride?" Artemis asked.

Alpheus shook his head. "I don't like heights."

"Oh," said Artemis. "Then how about Athena's offer to plant—"

"Don't like olives, either," he interrupted her to say before she could finish.

With a deep sigh, Artemis picked up her quiver. Reaching inside it, she pushed her silver arrows aside, then rummaged around till her fingers touched on

the gold figure of her three dogs. Reluctantly, she drew it out.

"The godboy Hephaestus made this," she told Alpheus, holding it out to him. "It's very special to me. But it's yours if you'll hand over Arethusa's cup and release her from that ridiculous promise you tricked her into making."

She didn't know if it was just her imagination, but she thought she saw a look of hurt flash in Alpheus's eyes at the words "ridiculous promise." But then his eyes brightened as she handed him the gold figure. "Wow, this is really nice! These are supposed to be your dogs, aren't they? They look like them."

Artemis nodded, watching Alpheus turn the figure over and over in his hands. "The details and the workmanship are amazing," he went on admiringly. But then he handed the figure back. "As beautiful

and valuable as it is, it's no substitute for the real thing, is it?"

*What?* Artemis hoped he didn't think she'd actually offer to give him any of her three dogs in trade. Because she'd *never* do that. Not in a bazillion years! She remembered him saying that he really wanted a dog of his own, only he couldn't take care of one, since he spent so much time in his river. Still, what if he'd changed his mind?

"I'm not giving you my actual dogs," she said, just to be clear.

"Wasn't gonna ask," he assured her, though she wasn't certain she believed that.

Wondering what in the world she could offer in trade now, Artemis slipped the gold figure back inside her quiver.

Just then Alpheus reached over and pulled one

of her silver arrows from the quiver before she could stop him. Toying with it, he slid his fingers down its length. "As goddessgirl of the hunt, you must be pretty good at archery," he commented.

*Huh? Has he been living under a rock in that river of his?* Artemis wondered. How could he not know that she and her brother Apollo were the best archers on Mount Olympus? Possibly in all the world! Not that long ago, in the first girls-only Olympic Games (officially called the Heraean Games, in honor of the goddess Hera, who was Zeus's wife and Athena's stepmom), Artemis had beat out some very skilled Amazonian and Norse archers to win the archery event. While shooting at flying targets, no less!

"Yeah, I'm pretty good," she told him with a smirk.

Still holding on to the arrow he'd picked up,

Alpheus jumped to his feet. "Show me," he said. He held out the arrow to her.

"Now?" she asked in surprise. Rising to her feet too, however, she took the arrow from him.

Alpheus grinned. Then he pointed to a willow tree about thirty feet down the bank. One long limb of the tree hung out over the river. "Tell you what," he said. "See that branch? The long one that extends over my river? If you can hit it with your arrow somewhere within a foot of its tip, then I'll release Arethusa from her promise and give up her cup."

"You will?" Artemis could hardly believe her good luck. What he'd requested was an easy-peasy shot for her. Good thing he didn't seem to realize just how expert an archer she was. But knowing how tricky he could be, she narrowed her eyes at him. "What's the catch?"

"No catch," Alpheus replied, blinking at her innocently. "But if you miss the shot, Arethusa's promise becomes yours."

Stunned, Artemis took a step back. "Ha!" she exclaimed. "You're so fickle you'd trade one girl for another as long as *someone* goes out with you?"

Alpheus shrugged. "If the girl was you, I would."

Artemis stared at the annoying boy. "You hardly even know me," she scoffed. "And . . . hello . . . *Arethusa*? What about her? I thought you liked her."

"I *know* you," he countered. "Enough to know you're awesome. And I . . . I think I kinda like you better than Arethusa now!"

"Oh, really?" She crossed her arms and stared at him scornfully.

Making puppy-dog eyes at her, he said, "You're something special, Artemis. If all the girls in the

world came together, I could pick you out of the bunch of them in a flash."

"What?" she asked.

"I give you my pledge that I could!" he insisted.

*Godsamighty!* thought Artemis. This river god was determined to get himself a girlfriend! But he was going about it all wrong. All at once, Aphrodite's words at dinner the night before came back to her: "I wonder why he thinks he needs to trick a girl into promising to go out with him. Seems oddly desperate."

"Why is getting a girl to go out with you so important, anyway?" she asked him. "And why are you in such a hurry?"

At her questions, he fell silent for a moment. His face turned pink and his eyes got shifty or maybe even distressed. What was up with that?

"It just is," he said finally. He looked at her with puppy-dog eyes again and smiled. "So, is it a deal? Will ya go for the shot?"

Artemis sighed in exasperation. For some unfathomable reason (unfathomable to her, anyway) Alpheus seemed to have become smitten with *her* now. She thought about telling him she already had a crush. But then she remembered that after last night's argument, she might not. Besides, she could fight her own battles. She didn't need to bring Actaeon into this dumb mess!

There was zero chance her arrow would miss that tree branch anyway, she thought. "Fine," she told him. "I accept your challenge."

# 9
## Shoot!

**ONCE ALPHEUS HAD RETURNED HER SILVER** arrow, she laid it on the ground like it was a starting line in a race.

"This will be my shooting line, okay?" she said to him.

"It's perfect," he replied. Then he sighed happily. "Just like you."

She rolled her eyes. What was it with this fickle guy? Like a river, his affections seemed to flow easily from girl to girl. After pulling another arrow from her quiver, she picked up her bow.

Stepping up to the arrow that was her shooting line, Artemis fitted the notched end of the second arrow into her bowstring. Before pulling back on the string, however, she checked to make sure that her deer, and any other animals that might be around, were far from the flight path her arrow would take. As any good archer knew, it was important to consider safety first. Even though her magic arrows could do no real harm, she didn't want to scare an animal!

By now her deer had moved several yards behind her to graze on a lush patch of grass. Not spying any other animals—including birds—in the area, she

eyed the end of the willow branch sticking out over the river.

Ready . . . aim . . .

She released her arrow. *Zzzing!* It shot straight and true, just as she'd trained it to do.

But a mere second before it could reach the branch, Alpheus threw both his arms high. In response, the water in the river below the branch rose straight up in a column. *Thwack!* Whiplike, the column of water lashed out to strike her arrow full force. The arrow was dashed to the ground before it could hit its mark!

"Oops!" Alpheus snickered. "Looks like you missed!"

Artemis scowled at him. "You cheated!" she argued through clenched teeth.

He shrugged. "Pretty cool trick, though, huh?"

Artemis just glared at him, frustrated and shocked by his feat. Normally, raising such a large column of water and flicking it like a whip would be something only Poseidon could do. Because he was the godboy of the sea! As far as she knew, river gods didn't—or shouldn't—possess that kind of power.

"It's a new ability. Super handy. Sort of came to me out of nowhere yesterday," he went on. "Helped me shift those trees that had fallen over from the windstorm."

*Arethusa's magic cup must've given him the ability to do what he just did!* Artemis thought. She crossed her fingers that he wouldn't realize this anytime soon. Otherwise there was no way he'd ever give the cup back. What if his powers continued to increase?

Might he one day use them to challenge Poseidon's right to rule the sea? That would upset the current balance of power. Which would *not* be a good thing. In fact, it was the kind of thing that would make Zeus furious. At her and the nymphs!

"You're not mad, are you?" Alpheus asked. "Because you look mad." He shrugged. "All's fair in love and war, right?"

*Grrr,* thought Artemis. She felt like punching him in the face. Still, violence rarely fixed anything. Promise or no promise, however, there was no way she would go out with this cheater. Still . . . the cup! Somehow she needed to get it.

To buy herself some time while she considered what to do, she said, "I still don't understand why this going-out promise is so important to you."

Alpheus frowned at her stubbornly. "Like I said,

it just is." His eyes went a little worried and shifty like maybe he was *afraid* to tell her the truth. Or just hugely embarrassed?

"Is there some particular reason you want a girlfriend so badly? And so fast?" she insisted, crossing her arms. "If you'd just tell me what it is, maybe we could come up with a way out of this for us both."

He made a scoffing noise and wouldn't meet her eyes. "A deal's a deal."

This was going nowhere. Suddenly Artemis remembered something. "You told Arethusa she had till five o'clock this afternoon to deliver on her promise," she reminded Alpheus. "So I demand the same terms." Then, hoping he really had no idea where his new power had come from, she added sternly, "And you need to hand over her cup. Now."

Sounding disappointed, and maybe a little

frustrated or even panicked for some reason, he blurted, "Yeah, I guess."

*Phew,* thought Artemis. Was it really going to be this easy? He must not have connected the cup with his increased power . . . *yet*. She slung her bow over her back, and then bent to pick up the arrow she'd used as a shooting line.

"I'll get your other one," Alpheus offered, as if hoping she might change her mind about waiting till five o'clock if he was helpful. Not going to happen!

"Sure, please. Go fetch!" she said to him as if he were one of her dogs.

"Arf! Arf!" he responded playfully. Then he trotted off after her arrow. He must have hidden the cup near the same willow tree she'd been trying to shoot. Because when he returned, he was carrying it. The arrow, though, was clenched in his teeth,

the same way one of her dogs would've fetched it for her.

She couldn't help laughing. This guy could be funny at times, she had to admit, but it still didn't make her want to go out with him.

When she reached to take the arrow and the cup from him, he went, "Grrr," and shook his head before finally opening his mouth. She giggled again at his goofy sense of humor as the arrow dropped into her hands. It kind of reminded her of how goofy Karya could be sometimes. She slid it back in her quiver with one hand, and reached greedily for the cup with her other.

To her dismayed disappointment, Alpheus whisked it away before she could touch it. "I've changed my mind. This cup is mine until our bargain is satisfied."

*Argh!* "How about this? You give me the cup and I'll give you the gold figure of my dogs to keep until my return," Artemis countered, desperately digging through her quiver for it. She *had* to get the magical cup back before he realized its power!

"Nuh-uh," said Alpheus. "You were willing to trade it earlier, so I doubt you'd come back for it. You can't trick me *that* easily! Besides, what's the big deal about this cup?"

Artemis opened her mouth to argue, but then closed it. She couldn't risk making him suspicious about why she wanted the cup so badly. "Suit yourself," she said as casually as she could manage. She shouldered her quiver, and then whistled for her deer.

"Seems a shame to have to make another trip back here in just a few hours," Alpheus said as the deer

magically attached themselves to her chariot again. "We could start our date now."

"Nope," Artemis said firmly.

He sighed. "Okay. At least it won't be long till you're back again. I've never been on a date, but I'm thinking we might, um, go eat at the Supernatural Market? Maybe watch the sunset, and then I could walk you back to the Academy?"

His cheeks had turned pink with embarrassment over his suggestions, as if he really just wanted the whole date thing to be over with. Well, then, why would he want to take her out at all? Whatever! She didn't have time to figure him out right now.

"We'll see," interrupted Artemis, before he could go on. *In your dreams* was what she was really thinking. She jumped into her chariot and took up the reins.

"Promise you won't be late, okay?" Alpheus said. The note of panic in his voice was unmistakable this time. Why was he so afraid she'd bail on him? He knew how responsible she was!

"I'll come at five, like I said." Then to her deer she chanted:

*"Chariot, chariot, rise away!*

*Take me back to MOA!"*

There, that was certainly a better magic chant than her last one!

"Later!" Alpheus shouted up to her as her deer and chariot rose. Then he splashed back into his river, taking Arethusa's magical cup with him.

Artemis only grunted in reply. On the short trip back to MOA she contemplated what to do next. She wasn't ready to face the nymphs until she figured out a plan. So once she was back at the Academy,

she'd send Arethusa a message instead. She hated to think how upset the nymph would be that Alpheus still had her cup. She'd surely be relieved to learn she was no longer obligated to go out with him, though. What would the nymphs think when they discovered Artemis had been tricked into taking over Arethusa's promise? *Argh!*

As soon as her chariot landed in the MOA courtyard, Artemis jumped down from it. She patted her deer and thanked them before they leaped away to park the chariot near the MOA stables and then go graze in the nearby gardens.

Once inside the Academy, she kept her head down as she took the steps two at a time up the marble staircase to the girls' dorm. She didn't want to talk to anyone right now, especially not Pheme. She was the goddessgirl of gossip and rumor, who

also attended MOA. Even when you were determined to keep something a secret, she could dig it out of you faster than Artemis's dogs could gobble snacks!

It didn't matter that Artemis had no intention of delivering on her promise to Alpheus. It would still be embarrassing for everyone to know about it. What would the nymphs think when they discovered she'd been tricked into taking over Arethusa's promise? What would her brother think? Or Actaeon? *Gulp*.

As often happened, Amby, Nectar, and Suez recognized Artemis's footsteps in the dorm hallway. They pawed at the door and whined in their eagerness to see her. "Stand back, boys," she called to them. Carefully opening the door a crack, she squeezed in through it.

Right away they leaped around her, licking her hands, her face, or whatever part of her was within easy reach. She squatted to ruffle their fur and hug them. There was nothing she could do that would ever change *their* good opinion of her, she thought. They would love and appreciate her no matter what!

After a while she stood again and shrugged off her bow and quiver. Before she tossed them onto her bed, she reached inside her quiver and pulled out the gold figure of her dogs. Despite the horrible situation she was in, she was glad Alpheus hadn't taken it in trade, since she really did love it and want to keep it.

Carefully Artemis placed the figure back on its shelf at the end of her bed. Then she threaded her way past all the messy piles on her floor to refill

her dogs' food and water bowls. While they were (not so patiently) taking turns scarfing down the new kibble and lapping up the fresh water, she sat down at her desk. After shoving aside some class textscrolls, a file for sharpening arrow tips, and miscellaneous old homework papers, she found a clean sheet of papyrus.

Additional searching yielded her favorite green feather pen. Quickly she wrote a message:

*Dear Arethusa,*

*Good news! Alpheus has released you from your promise to go out with him.*

(She left out any mention of him tricking *her* into taking over that promise. She'd save that information for later. Much later. Like maybe on the twelfth of never, if she could.)

*Although he hasn't yet yielded the cup, I have high hopes*

*he will. And here's another bit of good news. Luckily, he doesn't seem to realize it's magical. I plan to meet with him again at five o'clock today for further discussion. Will report back afterward.*

*Your loyal protector,*

*Artemis*

Even as she signed off, Artemis wondered how all of this was going to play out. Arethusa had insisted that Artemis was much cleverer than Alpheus, but what if the nymph was wrong? She'd always enjoyed the nymphs' good opinion of her and felt proud that she could help and protect them. But how could she be considered a good protector—much less their hero—if she couldn't even protect herself? Or convince Alpheus to give up Arethusa's magical cup, either?

Once her message was complete, the sheet of

papyrus magically rolled itself up into a notescroll. *Snap!* Digging around in a desk drawer, she located a length of red ribbon. She tied it around the notescroll, which she then carried to her open window. Leaning out over the sill, she called, "Magic breeze, come to me, please!"

No sooner were the words out of her mouth than a glittery breeze whooshed up to her window. "What may I do for thee?" it asked.

"Please deliver this notescroll to the nymph Arethusa," she told it.

"As you wish," the breeze consented breathily.

Thanking it, Artemis let go of the scroll, and watched it float out and away from the window. With little puffs, the magic breeze carried it off toward the olive grove and the trail.

She was just turning away from the window when there was a knock on her door.

"Artemis? Are you back?" Aphrodite's voice called out. "It's us, your besties!"

*Woof! Woof! Woof!* Amby, Nectar, and Suez ran to the door, wagging their tails. Although Aphrodite wasn't exactly a dog lover, as far as they were concerned, any friend of Artemis's was a friend of theirs.

"Coming!" Artemis called out. But before she could reach the door, the knob turned. Aphrodite, Persephone, and Athena spilled into her room.

# 10 Confession Time

For some reason, each of Artemis's best friends was holding a large square woven bin. "What are those for?" Artemis asked curiously. She could see they were empty.

"For you!" replied Athena.

"We're going to help you organize your room," Aphrodite added brightly. To avoid Artemis's dogs

jumping on her, she'd held back a little, letting Persephone and Athena go ahead of her. Aphrodite didn't dislike dogs, exactly, just the mess that went with them. As she'd told Artemis more than once, dirty paw marks and dog slobber did not mix with her fashionable outfits.

"I had these extra bins left over from my own recent room-reorganization project," Aphrodite went on. "So I decided I'd donate them to you."

"Um . . . thanks?" said Artemis. Helping her organize her messy room was something Aphrodite had been threatening—er, *offering* to do for a long time. She knew she should be grateful. It was just that she had so much on her mind right now—mostly to do with Alpheus and Arethusa.

As Aphrodite closed Artemis's door, Persephone set down her bin and crouched on the floor next

to Suez. "Hello, you. Who's a good boy?" she said, fondly ruffling the fur behind the bloodhound's large, droopy ears. *She* didn't mind a bit of dog-related mess.

Neither did Athena. When Amby stretched out on the floor and rolled over onto his back, Athena tossed her bin onto the spare bed. Then she knelt and scratched his belly.

Artemis corralled Nectar while the fastidious goddessgirl of love and beauty edged around the girls and dogs, heading with her bin toward the piles of clothes that Artemis hadn't yet found time to launder.

"Honestly, I don't know how you can live like this," Aphrodite said as she began tossing tights, chitons, and pj's into her bin.

Artemis opened her mouth to protest that some

of those things might be clean, but then closed it. Actually, all her clothes could probably use a good wash. She'd been thinking this for a while, of course, but there were so many other things to do that she just never got around to it.

She shrugged. "Hey! I'm not the messiest one around here, you know. You've seen Principal Zeus's office, right?"

Aphrodite grimaced, no doubt picturing the discarded Thunder Bar wrappers, empty Zeus Juice and *Zap*ple bottles, gym towels, files, maps, and scrollazines that always had to be brushed from chair seats before visiting students could even sit down in there.

"Zeus and I have similar styles of housekeeping," Artemis went on. "It works for him, and he's not just MOA's principal but also King of the Gods and

Ruler of the Heavens. So I've never seen any reason it can't work for me, too."

The girls all laughed at this, including Aphrodite.

"Hera made him clean up his office once, remember?" Athena commented as she picked up her storage bin and began to fill it with dog things: squeak toys and balls, leashes, and bags of dog food and dog treats. She left the dogs' food and water bowls where they were. "But it was back to its usual messy state soon enough," she added wryly.

Right away, Aphrodite cast a helpful magic spell upon the outfits she deemed worthy of cleaning and keeping.

*"Wash, dry, iron.*

*Clothes look like new!*

*Styles and colors sorted.*

*Then hung up too!"*

The clothes whirled and twirled, becoming magically clean. Then they flew around the room to sort themselves by style and color. Lastly, they hung themselves neatly in Artemis's closet. Excited by all the activity, Artemis's dogs barked and snapped at the clothes until they were finally shut up in the closet.

In the meantime, Persephone tackled Artemis's desk. "A lot of this stuff could be thrown away," she said as she sorted through old homework papers and projects. She glanced over at Artemis. "Do you want to tell me what to save and what to toss?"

"Nuh-uh," Artemis replied. "You can decide." To aid the cleaning effort, she picked up her bow and quiver from her desk and moved them to lean against the wall at the end of her bed. Uninterested in what the girls were doing now, Amby, Nectar, and Suez retreated to her spare bed and settled down for naps.

When Artemis turned around, Persephone was lifting a blanket from the floor. She pulled out a trash can from underneath it, crumpled up some papers, and deposited them in the mostly empty can.

"So that's where that trash can disappeared to!" Artemis exclaimed, which made the others snort and giggle.

"Sooo . . . ," Aphrodite said, gathering up the clothes she'd rejected and putting them into a bin marked "For Donation." "Which of our trade ideas did Alpheus go for?"

"He didn't go for any of them," Artemis admitted with a sigh. She was really reluctant to tell her BFFs how he'd tricked her. And how she was supposed to go out with him later this afternoon. But once she began her confession, the whole sorry story tumbled out.

"How dare he!" Persephone huffed when Artemis was almost to the end of her retelling. "He's despicable!"

"Absolutely!" Athena agreed emphatically.

Aphrodite dropped more items she'd weeded from Artemis's clothes pile into the now overflowing donation bin. When she turned back to face Artemis, her blue eyes sparked with anger.

"The Supernatural Market? A sunset walk to the Academy? Sounds like he wants to show off to everyone that he's got a date. Ha! No way are you going out with that . . . that . . . *sneaky snake*!" she hissed.

"Good thing Medusa didn't hear you say that," Artemis joked, trying to lighten the mood. A mortal student here at MOA, Medusa had a dozen wiggly snakes for hair. She treated them as pets and had

even given them icky-cute names including Viper, Slither, and Wiggle!

With a deep sigh, Artemis grew solemn. "That isn't even the worst of it," she told her friends. "Turns out that Arethusa's cup—the one I told you about at dinner yesterday—possesses magic."

All three of her BFFs gasped upon hearing this information.

"I didn't know till Arethusa told me this morning, but I'm positive that's what allowed Alpheus to knock down my arrow," Artemis went on. "He hasn't yet figured out his new power comes from the cup, but once he does, he'll try to keep it for sure."

Hearing this, worried looks came over her friends' faces. "Ye gods," said Persephone. "That's not good!"

"Not at all," Aphrodite agreed. "If that happens, his power could grow even stronger!"

Athena frowned. “I wonder if my dad knows about Arethusa’s cup.”

“Think we should tell him?” Artemis asked. She had mixed feelings about that idea. On the one hand, it would be embarrassing to tell Principal Zeus her story. What if he started to think her unqualified to protect the nymphs? On the other hand, he’d almost certainly be able to sort things out, which would be a relief. But on the third hand (if she’d had one), she should try to solve her own problems, right? Unlike the nymphs, she didn’t want to constantly run to someone else for help. Not until her own best efforts had failed, anyway.

“Dad and Hera left after breakfast to take Hebe to this big toddler park in Athens,” Athena informed her friends. Hebe was Athena’s adorable little half sister. “It could be hours before they’re back.” She

paused, looking at the others. "We could send him a message by magic breeze, though. Or—"

"Or we could try to deal with it ourselves," Aphrodite interrupted her to finish. "After all, we do have immortal powers equal to Alpheus's. We need to fix this situation fast, though, before he realizes the cup can increase his power beyond ours."

"You took the words right out of my mouth," Persephone said with a grin.

Artemis nodded. "Mine too." Now that they'd finished organizing her room, the four goddessgirls sat in a circle on the newly free-of-junk rug between her two beds.

"One thing is for sure," Aphrodite told Artemis firmly. "We're coming with you to your next meeting with Alpheus."

Although Artemis had reservations about her

three friends coming with her, she was touched that her failed Alpheus mission didn't seem to have made them think any less of her. The way they were rallying around her with their full support made her feel truly grateful. "You guys are the best, you know that, right?" she told them.

"Of course we do," Aphrodite said with a straight face. Then she giggled.

"Okay, let's do this!" Athena exclaimed, a determined gleam lighting her gray-blue eyes. "All we need is a plan!"

"Yes, a No Date/No Cup for Alpheus Plan!" added Persephone.

"Hold on a sec," Artemis protested. "As much as I appreciate your offer of help, this is my problem, not yours. You don't need to get involved. I don't want Alpheus tricking any of you, too. I'd feel just awful!"

Aphrodite jutted out her chin. "We're going with you and that's that. You can't stop us."

"Agreed," said Persephone. "Unlike your dogs, we don't obey *stay* commands."

This made them all laugh. "Okay," said Artemis. "I give up. Thanks, you guys." Knowing that she was no longer in this thing alone caused her spirits to rise, even if there wasn't a plan yet. She got to her feet. "I need to take my dogs outside before we grab lunch."

"We'll all come," her three friends chorused, then laughed at how alike their thinking was. The four goddessgirls started downstairs with Artemis's dogs trotting along behind them.

"Hey, there's something I wanted to ask you about," Persephone said to Artemis once they were all outside in the courtyard. "Is something up with

Actaeon? Usually he's pretty chill. But ever since yesterday, Hades said he's been acting like he's angry about something."

The girls all glanced at Artemis. Watching her dogs scamper off to sniff around the edges of the courtyard, she suddenly had the uneasy feeling that her friends had discussed this among themselves earlier. They'd only been waiting for the right time to ask her about it.

"Any idea what could be bothering him?" Athena pushed.

Artemis thought about what had happened between her and Actaeon last night and a hard knot formed in her stomach. "It's my fault!" she blurted out. "I'm pretty sure he doesn't want to be my crush anymore."

"What? That can't be true," Aphrodite said at once.

"Yeah, that boy looks at you like you hung the moon," said Athena. "Which sort of makes sense since you *are* goddessgirl of the moon."

Persephone snickered and nodded. "Yeah, Hades said Actaeon's face always *lights up* when Apollo mentions you or tells stories about you."

They all groaned at her pun, but the *light*hearted conversation was lifting Artemis's mood. Her friends could always be counted on to do that.

"Embarrassing stories, no doubt," she couldn't help remarking. Which was likely how Actaeon had found out about her lousy sense of direction, she thought for the second time.

Artemis felt Aphrodite's eyes on her as the four-some walked across the courtyard to her dogs. Then the girls began to circle the grassy area at the edge of it with the dogs following. "What makes you think

Actaeon wants to un-crush you?" Aphrodite asked at last. "Did you two have a fight?"

Leave it to the goddessgirl of love to pick up on possible reasons for cracks in a relationship, Artemis thought. Just like she'd done back in her room, she soon found herself telling her friends stuff she'd never intended to reveal to anyone. And just like always, they were wonderfully sympathetic.

When Artemis described her jealous outburst at the Supernatural Market, after Actaeon had performed his drinking-straw trick for another girl, Athena, Aphrodite, and Persephone all reminded her of their own past episodes of jealousy.

"We've all been there. Remember how I was jealous of my baby sister when she was first born?" Athena said with an embarrassed groan. "Now I think she's adorable."

"And remember that time I got crazy jealous of Eos for going to Ares's room? Turned out he just wanted her to get rid of a spider because he's scared of them and didn't want me to know!" said Aphrodite. Eos, goddessgirl of the dawn, wasn't afraid of spiders or bugs of any kind, due to her friendship with a mortal boy who was obsessed with insect life.

"And not that long ago, I was jealous of Minthe," Persephone reminded Artemis. "It made me *so* mad that she kept flirting with Hades. Even though he didn't return her affections."

Minthe, a water nymph, had been in charge of a river in the Underworld at the time, so she'd been around Hades often. Now she was caretaker of a fountain on the grounds of MOA, and, luckily, she'd transferred her feelings for Hades to a boy who liked her back.

Artemis could feel the knot in her stomach gradually start to unwind as she and her friends discussed their past jealousies. She described her conversation with Actaeon on the archery field yesterday evening, relating how he'd seemed to take offense at her efforts to help Arethusa. It was a relief to unburden herself.

Afterward, Aphrodite gave some relationship advice. "Being mortal, Actaeon can have no idea of the responsibilities goddesses and gods have to shoulder. You're different from him in that way and always will be. It's just something you'll both have to accept."

"It's the same thing with Heracles and me," said Athena, referring to her superstrong mortal crush. "We try to work out the kinks in our immortal-mortal relationship as we go along."

"In spite of what Actaeon thinks, I'm sure Arethusa and your other nymph friends appreciate your help," said Persephone. "You're a hero to them!"

"Well, I used to be. Not so much lately," Artemis said doubtfully. She was remembering how Arethusa had fainted when she'd found out that Artemis had failed to solve all her problems during her first meeting with Alpheus. Not to mention how Dicte had practically accused her of neglecting her goddess duty as protector of nymphs. And although it was true that she'd finally managed to help where the promise was concerned, it was only at cost to herself!

Had Actaeon been right? Were her efforts so far just making things worse? If she hadn't taken on Arethusa's boy trouble, was it possible that the

nymphs would have found a way to solve that problem themselves? But then again, what if they hadn't been able to? Well, at the very least she was saving them the frustration of having to meet directly with Alpheus.

The goddessgirls discussed all this as they circled the courtyard several times. Artemis kept an eye on her dogs as they went, allowing them to wander short distances away to sniff at interesting smells. The girls had just moved back to the topic of a No Date/No Cup for Alpheus Plan when it was time to head back to the cafeteria for lunch.

"Instead of making him dig in his heels as you feared earlier, Artemis, maybe a meeting with all of us at once will have the opposite effect," Persephone said as they crossed the courtyard. "Maybe having to face *four* goddessgirls will be enough to intimidate

him into agreeing to drop the promise and give up the cup."

"Hope so," Artemis said. "He's pretty stubborn, though." As they started up the Academy's granite steps, she tuned out the rest of what her friends were saying. Because she suddenly glimpsed Actaeon! He was sitting on a bench sharpening the tip of an arrow in a far corner of the courtyard, half hidden behind a large planter of tall crocuses and daffodils. A half-eaten sandwich lay on the bench next to him, probably his lunch. Since he was turned sideways from them, he hadn't noticed her.

Even from this distance she could see that the arrow he held was not one of his usual ones. It was quite short, for one thing. And it was bright green.

She stared at his profile. *Sigh.* He was sooo cute. Never had she liked a boy this much. For a

moment, she considered going over to talk to him. But what could she say if he asked about Arethusa and Alpheus? There was no way she wanted him to know how horribly she'd messed up. And if there was still a chance he wanted them to be crushes, it would definitely not help their relationship for him to find out that Alpheus had transferred his crush—as well as the date promise—to *her*!

Quickening her step, Artemis followed her friends and dogs up the steps to the Academy's bronze doors.

# 11
## Emergency Meeting

AFTER TAKING HER DOGS UP TO HER ROOM, Artemis rejoined her three friends in the cafeteria for lunch. Athena, Persephone, and Aphrodite had already begun to discuss possible ideas for dealing with that tricky river godboy.

"So when the four of us confront Alpheus, what are we going to do or say, exactly?" Persephone asked.

"Maybe a good talking-to will be all that's needed," suggested Athena, opening a carton of nectar.

"Or I could cast a spell to make him fall in love with some other girl," Aphrodite mused as she used her fork to spear a cherry tomato from her salad.

"But that wouldn't really be fair to the other girl, would it?" Persephone pointed out.

Aphrodite shrugged. "Hmm. I guess you're right."

"Remember that he's a godboy and so could fight our spells with his own," Artemis reminded them. "And we don't know how powerful his magic may be now that he's got Arethusa's cup."

"Good point," said Athena. "And we definitely don't want to do anything that might tip him off that the cup is the source of his new powers!"

By the time they'd finished eating, they still

hadn't come up with a solid plan. So they decided to hope that intimidating Alpheus into behaving would succeed.

They were taking their trays to the tray return when a magic breeze whooshed into the cafeteria, causing everyone's hair, tunics, and chitons to flutter. "Artemis, art thou present?" it asked.

As other students looked on with interest, Artemis waved to the breeze. "Over here!"

Huffing and puffing with great effort, it blew over to her and dropped a conch shell onto her tray. *Thonk!*

"Whoa!" said Artemis. The shell was so heavy it almost knocked the tray from her hands. Luckily, she managed to rebalance before it (and everything on it) could clatter to the floor.

"Conch shells!" the breeze grumbled in disgust.

"Wouldn't thou thinkest a sea nymph could use note-scrolls for messages like everyone else? But *nooo*!" Then it whirled around in a huff and whooshed back out of the cafeteria.

After setting her tray in the return, Artemis picked up the shell. "*Whoa!* This thing *is* heavy! I'm surprised that breeze was able to lug it all this way."

"Winds can be strong when they must," Athena noted.

"Hold it up to your ear and see what it says. Since it's from a sea nymph, it's probably from Arethusa," Aphrodite said as she set her own tray in the return.

Aphrodite was born from sea foam. Maybe when she was younger she'd also communicated using shells, Artemis thought. Putting a finger to her lips to signal for quiet, she held the shell at her ear to listen.

Immediately, Arethusa's voice drifted out of the conch, too soft for her friends to hear. "Got your message, Artemis. Please meet me and the other nymphs in our forest right away. It's an emergency!" The minute the nymph's message ended, the shell disappeared into thin air. *Plink!*

Artemis figured that her expression as she'd listened to the message must've shown her concern, because her friends' eyes had gone wide.

"What did she say?" asked Persephone.

"Emergency meeting," Artemis told the others.

"Emergency?" Athena repeated. "Uh-oh. Think the nymphs know what happened with you and Alpheus this morning?" She and Persephone quickly set their trays in the return too, and the girls all rushed for the exit.

Artemis scrunched up her face. "I don't see how.

But just before you all came to help clean up my room, I did send a notescroll to let her know that Alpheus had released her from her promise." She bit her lip before adding, "I didn't tell her the rest, though. I was too embarrassed to admit that he'd tricked me into making the very same promise. I'm supposed to be smarter than that!" She groaned.

"Could've happened to any of us," Persephone consoled her. "Don't beat yourself up over it—just move forward." And the four girls did just that, moving all the way out of the cafeteria.

In the hallway, Aphrodite glanced at the others. "Winged sandals will get us to the nymphs faster than if we walk."

"Agreed," said Athena. "C'mon."

The goddessgirls hurried over to the big basket of winged sandals by MOA's front doors and each chose

a pair. Then they shucked off their regular sandals and left them by the door before slipping the winged sandals onto their feet. Instantly, the sandals' straps twined around their ankles, and the silver wings at the sandals' heels began to flap. With their feet several inches above the ground, they zipped out the Academy's bronze doors.

As they sped across the courtyard, Artemis noticed that Actaeon no longer sat on the bench outside. She hadn't seen him in the cafeteria, either. But since he'd been eating a sandwich when she saw him, he'd probably gotten it from the snack table earlier. She briefly wondered where he'd gone as the girls' sandals whisked them through the olive grove at the side of the courtyard and around the looped trail.

When they reached the forested place where Arethusa was staying with her tree-nymph friends,

the goddessgirls skidded to a stop. After loosening their sandals' straps, they looped them over the silver wings to hold them still.

Right away, Arethusa swung down from the trees to stand on the ground. She was quickly joined by Pitys, Dicte, Karya, and Syke, their pale faces all glowing like fairy lights.

"Hooray! You're here!" Arethusa shouted. She gave Artemis a big hug.

Artemis was a little surprised at this enthusiastic greeting, since her letter to Arethusa this morning had clearly indicated she hadn't yet retrieved the magic cup. Before asking about that, she introduced her BFFs, though it wasn't really necessary. The nymphs knew all about them from stories Artemis had shared. And, of course, the nymphs were also avid readers of *Teen Scrollazine*!

"Thank you for what you did for me!" Arethusa went on to Artemis. "It was supersweet of you to offer yourself in my place. To take over the promise Alpheus tricked me into making."

"Huh?" said Artemis. "Who told you about that?"

"Pheme," answered Pitys, flipping a lock of her blue-green hair over one shoulder.

Though Artemis and her BFFs were fond of Pheme, they simultaneously rolled their eyes at this news.

*That gossipy goddessgirl!* Artemis huffed to herself. How in the world could Pheme have found out? And so fast, too!

"Figures she was responsible," said Aphrodite. "But as usual, she only got part of the story correct."

"Yeah, she left out the shooting challenge," said Persephone. "Or maybe she just didn't know about it."

"Shooting challenge?" echoed Syke. The nymphs' foreheads wrinkled in confusion.

Before Artemis could explain, however, the girls all heard the flutter of wings overhead and looked up.

It was Pheme herself! Flapping her small, glittery orange wings, she settled to the ground among them. It was as if she'd been waiting close by in order to make an entrance once Artemis and her friends arrived. Which meant she knew they'd be coming. But how?

"Hi, there." Pheme greeted Artemis and the others with a quick wave. "Arethusa mentioned she was going to hold an emergency meeting here. I thought my readers should be in the know, so here I am, reporting for *Teen Scrollazine*!" As usual, her words puffed from her orange-glossed lips to rise above her head in little cloud letters before fading away.

This was a useful gift, as it allowed the girl to circulate her gossip more widely.

Arethusa nodded, but before she could speak, Pheme chattered on to Artemis. "I expect you're wondering how I found out about the problems between you and Alpheus?"

Frowning, Artemis tried to get a word in edgewise. "Uh-huh, but you didn't—"

Before she could finish protesting that Pheme hadn't gotten the details of her story entirely correct, Pheme interrupted her. "Okay, so here's what happened. I was flying down by the river about an hour ago when I heard Alpheus cheerfully singing."

"Yeah, I just bet he was, that trickster," Aphrodite muttered, scowling.

Pheme's eyes flicked over to her, but her words

didn't slow. "I followed the sound of his voice and called down to him, 'You sound happy.' 'I am!' he shouted back. 'Any particular reason?' I asked him."

She paused for a second to look around at her rapt listeners before going on. "Well, you know how good I am at getting people to share information," she stated matter-of-factly. "So within minutes, Alpheus spilled the beans. Told me that 'the goddessgirl of the hunt' had promised to go out with him this very afternoon!"

Artemis tried to interrupt again to set the story straight. "Wait, that's not—"

Pheme was on a roll, however. She wasn't about to let go of her audience. Not even for a single second. "Well, I was certainly surprised to hear that!" she said, ignoring Artemis's attempt to sidetrack her tale.

"So I asked him, 'Why would she do that? Everyone knows she's crushing on Actaeon. Although he has been acting kind of sad today, so did they break up?'"

She looked in question at Artemis.

Artemis shot her another dark frown. She wasn't at all pleased by this obvious attempt to find out what was going on between her and Actaeon.

Pheme got the message and rushed on. "And that's when Alpheus explained that Artemis had agreed to rescue a wooden cup for Arethusa by taking the nymph's place and going out with him." Turning back to Artemis again, Pheme's brown eyes shone. "As you can imagine, I wasted no time in finding Arethusa after that. I wanted her to know what a hero you are!"

*Ye gods,* thought Artemis. Pheme's version of events was so annoying! She made it sound like

Artemis had sacrificed herself for Arethusa. In a way, she guessed she had, but the truth was more complicated. She opened her mouth to protest that she was no hero, but before she could, Arethusa struck a dramatic pose and raised the back of one hand to her forehead.

*Uh-oh. Is she going to faint again?* Before Artemis could hurry to her side just in case, Arethusa straightened. Eyeing Artemis, she smiled bravely. Her voice quavered only slightly as she said, "Alas, I can't let you take my place. 'Twould be unfair to you."

Artemis had had enough. "This is ridiculous. I'm no hero!" she exclaimed. In a rush of words, she confessed to the others what she'd already shared with her BFFs, telling them the whole story of her last meeting with Alpheus. She even added details she'd left out the first time about what she and Alpheus

had said to each other. Her listeners were all ears, especially Pheme. That girl had pulled out a papyrus pad and was even taking notes!

As Artemis's tale drew to a close, Athena piped up. "You don't think you're a hero? I disagree," she said firmly. "It took courage to confront Alpheus and try to make him see reason. I admire you for it—and so does everyone else."

At this there was a chorus of "yeah!" from goddessgirls and nymphs alike. Some even punched the air with their fists or clapped for her.

Aphrodite nodded, her eyes meeting Artemis's. "When Arethusa needed help, you didn't back down from trouble."

"Exactly," said Persephone. "You tried your best to right a wrong."

Arethusa smiled at Artemis. "I couldn't agree

more. You *are* my hero, even if that wily Alpheus did manage to trick you, too."

"Right!" said Pitys, with a nod. "I mean, how were you to know that Alpheus had gained the power to raise the river's water high enough to dash your arrow to the ground?"

Syke's fingers toyed nervously with the cute necklace of figs she'd worn today. "Do you think he's figured out by now that the *cup* gave him that magic power?" (Artemis had told everyone she feared this could happen.)

"We'd all better hope not!" Dicte declared. She twisted a short strand of her cherry-red hair worriedly.

Karya, who'd been holding and petting little Chester while listening to the conversation, sighed and set the puppy down now. "Alpheus must really like you," she said to Artemis a little sadly.

Aphrodite casually nudged Artemis and then nodded meaningfully toward Karya. Wiggling her eyebrows, she whispered a single word out of the side of her mouth. It was only loud enough for Artemis to hear. "Crushing," she said.

Artemis blinked. *Huh?* But then she remembered Karya's comments about Alpheus over the last couple of days. "I think he's dreamy." And "Alpheus should look for a girl who really likes him." When Arethusa had replied that Alpheus might have to look far and wide, and the other nymphs had giggled, Karya had just smiled goofily and replied, "You never know. I bet lots of girls like him."

Maybe not *lots* of girls, Artemis thought now. But one girl for sure. Aphrodite was right. Karya had a crush on the river god!

"Alpheus must *really* like you," Karya went on

to Artemis. "Or he wouldn't have pledged that he could pick you out in a flash from among all the girls in the world."

After repeating this detail from Artemis's story, Karya scuffed at the ground with one slender bare foot. "Not that you look like anyone else, of course," she added. "I mean, not every girl always carries a bow and quiver of arrows."

The things Karya said caused something to click inside Artemis's brain. Suddenly she got an idea for a way to fix things! She started to blurt it out, but then thought better of it. Instead, she leaned over to Arethusa and whispered, "Huh, just imagine if a crowd of girls showed up and he actually did have to pick me out. Think he could?" She waited, hoping Arethusa would catch on.

Arethusa cocked her head and stared at Artemis,

her attention captured. "I don't know. Maybe," she whispered back. "He *said* he could." She paused, appearing to ponder the matter. "No. Wait. He *pledged* he could pick you out . . . from all the girls in the world." All at once her face lit up. "That's a lot of girls. And a pledge is just a fancier word for a promise!"

She grabbed Artemis and hugged her, twirling her around. "That's it! Our way out of this!" she exclaimed. "You're a genius!"

Pulling back slightly, Artemis pretended confusion. "Who . . . me?"

"Yep!" Arethusa turned to the others, who all appeared to be genuinely puzzled. "Alpheus is not going out with *anyone* tonight," she declared. "Also, I've just figured out how we'll get him to return my magic cup!"

Artemis watched in relief as, with a confidence Artemis hadn't seen in the nymph since Alpheus had tricked her, Arethusa added, "Here's what we're going to do." Beaming from ear to ear, she told the whole group of nymphs and goddessgirls her plan. Everyone caught on fast—even Pheme was excited to help and not just gossip about it!—and began making suggestions for improvement. Turns out, the plan was exactly what Artemis had hoped Arethusa would come up with, because Artemis had (secretly) thought of it first.

Once everything was figured out, the goddessgirls and nymphs were all mightily satisfied. Because their plan was . . . *brilliant*!

# 12
## The Brilliant Plan

WITH NOT A MOMENT TO SPARE, THE FIVE nymphs and five goddessgirls (including Pheme) got to work. There was a lot to be done to implement their brilliant plan. In just four hours it would be five o'clock. Meeting time!

While Pheme flew here and there, puffing out invitations to other nymphs to join in their scheme,

Artemis, Arethusa, and the others began gathering or making the props they would need to carry it out. When all was ready, they marched down to the spot at the river where Artemis and Alpheus were to meet, arriving a good twenty minutes early to have time to prepare.

By now, Artemis and her three BFFs had dressed themselves in gowns borrowed from the nymphs. Their own chitons, which were finer and more colorful than the gowns of the nymphs, would have too easily marked them out to Alpheus as goddesses. Which was definitely not part of the plan!

After moving to stand at the river's edge, each girl bunched up her hair and tucked it under a cap woven from plant fibers Persephone had collected from the forest. Athena, goddessgirl of crafts, invention, wisdom, and weaving had taught the nymphs

to quickly make these simple caps. They weren't exactly designer but would do the trick of hiding everyone's hair color and style, helping to disguise their identities.

The cap-making crew had made plenty of extras. They handed them out as more and more nymphs arrived, summoned by Pheme's invitation. They'd been only too happy to help Artemis. She'd always been their protector too, after all!

"Echo! You came!" Artemis shouted when she caught sight of one particular nymph. Everyone's eyes were drawn to this famous nymph fashion designer's fabulous chiton. Flowy and turquoise, with sparkling gems along its three-layered, flounced hem, it was as amazing as anything Aphrodite might wear. It kind of reminded Artemis of a frosted turquoise cake!

"Well, of course I did," Echo replied as they hugged. "You've helped many a nymph at one time or another. Now we finally have a chance to return the favor!"

Her kind words made Artemis a little misty-eyed. "Thanks," she said. "Love your gown. It's going to get very messy soon, though. You know that, right?"

Echo laughed. "No problem. It's made of a magical fabric that's self-cleaning!"

"Awesome!" said Artemis. She'd have to look into those further!

They both joined in to help where they could as preparations continued. Though reluctant to be parted from her bow and arrows, Artemis knew they'd make her instantly recognizable to Alpheus. So she stashed them for safekeeping under a bush set back from the bank of his river. The goddessgirls

placed their winged sandals there too, going barefoot like the nymphs. Although her three BFFs carefully placed their folded-up chitons atop their sandals, Artemis haphazardly stuffed hers inside her quiver.

Then, giggling, the goddessgirls and nymphs scooped up handfuls of mud from the edge of the river and smeared it over their faces, arms, legs, and gowns to further disguise themselves.

"This river's mud has unique ingredients that will be good for our complexions," Aphrodite assured everyone.

"And it'll hide our shimmery skin, too," Athena noted.

Although they were on a tight schedule, somehow everything was ready in the nick of time. A hush fell over the group of fifty or so goddessgirls and nymphs as they waited for their plan to unfold.

At five o'clock on the dot, a whirlpool formed not far from shore and Alpheus rose up through its center. Naturally, he appeared startled to come face-to-face with fifty girls lined up in rows on the riverbank. "What's this? What's going on?" he asked in dismay.

Part of their plan required that Artemis and Arethusa not speak, since that could cause him to recognize their voices. The other girls had agreed to remain silent too. In fact, it had been decided that only Pitys would speak, and she stepped forward to do so now.

"Alpheus!" she called out in her lovely, clear voice. "I'm told that you made a pledge to the goddessgirl Artemis that you could pick her out in a flash from among all the girls of the world. Since there are only about fifty of us here, picking her out should be even easier-peasier."

"Hmm," said Alpheus. "Guess I *did* say that. Is this some kinda clever trick, Artemis?"

His narrowed eyes scanned the group of girls as he spoke, undoubtedly hoping she would react and give herself away when he said her name. But like all the rest except Pitys, Artemis stood still and kept mum.

"If you cannot pick her out," Pitys went on, "it's only fair that failing your pledge to do so should cancel out the promise she made to you. Agreed?"

Alpheus shrugged, looking like he wanted to argue, but was unable to reasonably do so. Especially when faced with an army of girls! "Yeah, I s'pose." Then he grinned. "Only there's no way I'm gonna fail, because—"

Before he could finish whatever he'd been about to say, Pitys added hurriedly, "And if you fail, you'll also have to give Arethusa back her cup."

Alpheus blinked in surprise, and then scanned the crowd, looking a little shamefaced. "Are you here too, Arethusa? Where are you? Speak up." When none of the girls moved or replied, he said apologetically, "I hope you're not mad that I changed my mind and started to like Artemis better than you."

"Ha!" said Pitys. "Don't flatter yourself. She couldn't care less! No one likes someone who bargains as unfairly as you have." The other girls all nodded their heads.

Alpheus's cheeks reddened with embarrassment.

"Well?" Pitys said. "What about the cup?"

Regaining his composure, Alpheus said, "Fine. If I fail, which I won't, I'll also return the cup. Let's just hurry this along, 'kay?"

*Phew,* thought Artemis. If he was agreeing so readily, it meant he hadn't yet worked out that

Arethusa's cup was the source of his increased power. And for some reason he was in a hurry, which worked in their favor.

Alpheus's eyes roamed over the fifty girls again. "Finding you isn't gonna be hard, Artemis," he said. "Once I wash away all that mud!"

So saying, he raised his arms in the air, preparing to make the river rise, Artemis was certain. But, of course, she had told the others how he'd brought up a column of river water to dash her arrow aside. She hadn't been ready for his maneuver the first time, but this time things were different. This time the girls had a plan!

In low voices, the entire group broke their silence at last and began to chant in harmony:

*"Supple branch and twisty vine,*

*Come at once, this boy entwine!"*

They spoke in unison to keep up their disguises. But truthfully, the only voice necessary to perform the spell was Persephone's. As the goddessgirl of spring and growing things, all plants eagerly obeyed her every command.

*Snap! Crack! Ssslither!* Instantly, the branches of nearby trees and vines lengthened and grew, extending their reach toward Alpheus. Within seconds they'd wrapped him in their embrace, at the same time bringing down his arms and binding them tightly to his sides.

Alpheus grunted and spat a leaf from his mouth. "Cheaters!" he yelled.

"He looks like a grumpy green mummy!" Artemis whispered out of one side of her mouth to Aphrodite. The two of them were standing next to each other in a middle row. They almost cracked up, but luckily

were able to control themselves and avoid drawing the river god's attention.

*Arf! Arf!* Suddenly Karya's little brown-and-white puppy, Chester, appeared on the trail above the river. Most of the girls in the group managed not to automatically turn to look. Like Artemis, they just shifted their eyes toward the sound. Although Karya had left the pup in a safe place back on the upper trail, he must have gotten tired of waiting, escaped, and decided to come fetch her. Now he scampered down to the riverbank and sniffed cautiously at the strange, green-wrapped boy.

"Nice doggie," Alpheus said. His eyes, peeking out from all the green, glinted with glee. "Artemis likes dogs. I met three of them just yesterday, but I didn't see you. Are you her new puppy?"

*Arf!* Chester barked. Then he wagged his tail.

Though he hadn't understood a word of what Alpheus had said to him, he obviously sensed that the river god meant him no harm. That Alpheus was, in fact, quite fond of dogs, as Artemis knew.

"Good boy," Alpheus said. He tossed his head toward the group of girls. "Go find Artemis, 'kay?"

Chester hesitated, looking back and forth between the nice green mummy and the mud-faced girls.

"Go on. Go, boy!" Alpheus encouraged him. "She's waiting for you to play!"

Seeming to understand a little of what Alpheus wanted him to do, Chester trotted over to the girls. He circled the group, sniffing at each in turn. Then all at once he ran to a girl in the very back row. *Arf! Arf!* He leaped around her and pawed at her gown until she finally stooped to pick him up.

Alpheus laughed. "You!" he said, tossing his head

in the girl's direction since he was unable to point. "You're Artemis!"

But it was Karya, of course.

"Wrong! You lose!" the real Artemis sang out, stepping away from the group. She whipped off her cap to reveal her glossy black hair, then wiped some of the mud from her face with both hands.

Laughing and chatting in relief now that Alpheus had been defeated, the nymphs and goddessgirls all waded knee-deep into the river. There they washed the mud from themselves as best they could.

Pheme had watched the whole drama unfolding while fluttering above a small tree to one side of all the girls. Now she flew off, looking excited. Artemis fully expected that the goddessgirl of gossip's account of what had happened would appear in

the very next issue of *Teen Scrollazine*. Just how much of it would be accurate was anyone's guess, however.

Meanwhile, Persephone spoke a reverse spell that caused the branches and vines binding Alpheus to unwind, shorten, and retreat. Curiously, as soon as he was free, he glanced up at the sky and studied the sun's position as if to determine the time.

"Woo-hoo!" he shouted, doing a little happy dance. "It's five fifteen. And I'm still me!" Then Artemis thought she heard him grumble, "That dumb ol' Poseidon."

*Huh?* Had he worried the branches and vines binding him might've turned him into a plant or something? she wondered. And what did Poseidon or the time have to do with anything?

True to his word, when Arethusa went over to ask

for her cup, Alpheus pointed her toward the river-bank. "It's at the base of that big rock," he told her without hesitation. She raced over immediately and gave a whoop of delight when she found her cup where he'd said it would be.

To Artemis's surprise, the river god didn't look at all upset over its loss. Nor did he retreat to his river right away. Instead, when Karya threw a stick for Chester and it landed at Alpheus's feet, he picked it up and tossed it for the dog, joining in the game.

Gradually, after hugs and fond farewells, most of the nymphs began to head out. Echo hugged Artemis again as she prepared to leave for her tree-house home in Boeotia. "There's going to be a fashion show at Hera's shop in the Immortal Marketplace in a couple of weeks," she told Artemis. "Some of my

designs will be included. Maybe you and your besties would like to come? I could send you invitations."

"Fantastic!" Artemis said. "We'd love to come!" Even though fashion wasn't her thing, she'd enjoy going to the show with her friends and hanging out with Echo again. She couldn't wait to tell Aphrodite. When she heard about it, she'd be over-the-top excited.

Arethusa, Syke, Dicte, and Pitys stuck around longer than most of the other nymphs. When they were finally ready to take off, Artemis hugged Arethusa first, saying, "I'm so glad you got your magic cup back. And, um, sorry I wasn't that much help."

"Oh, but you were!" Arethusa told her, doing a gleeful little twirl. "Because when I found out you'd taken over my promise, I realized it wasn't fair to rely on you so much. Sometimes I need to solve my own problems."

"Right. It's not fair of any of us to expect you to fix *everything*," added Dicte. For once, she looked completely earnest and not at all frowny. "You always do your best for us. It was wrong of me to ever doubt that."

Pitys and Syke nodded in agreement. "We're so lucky Karya remembered about Alpheus's pledge to you," Pitys said.

Syke grinned. "It was exactly the information Arethusa needed to come up with a plan."

Arethusa nodded.

"And we're lucky so many nymphs pitched in to help, too," added Artemis.

Indeed, things had worked out better than she could ever have imagined. It seemed likely that from here on out these nymphs would try to take more responsibility for themselves and their problems. *Phew!* That was a relief. Still, she'd always be there

when they truly needed her, and would forever remain their devoted protector.

Now Syke, Dicte, and Pitys each hugged Artemis in turn. No one minded the mud that still clung to their clothing, since they were all in the same condition. But afterward Artemis said, "I guess my friends and I need to give you back your gowns."

Having just come over to stand nearby, Aphrodite overheard. "I can cast a spell to clean up our borrowed clothes, but let's wait till we're back at MOA so we can shower before changing back into our own gowns." She offered to magically clean the gowns the nymphs were wearing too, but they insisted it wasn't necessary. "We'll shower before we change too," Pitys told her. "At our favorite hidden waterfall."

"And there's no hurry to return the gowns," Syke added. "We have plenty."

After Artemis bid good-bye to Arethusa, Dicte, Syke, and Pitys, she went to the bush where she'd stashed her bow and quiver of arrows. She slung the quiver over her back along with her bow. As she put on her winged sandals, she noticed that her three besties had wandered down to the river to watch some orange-beaked white swans swimming by. "Ready to go?" she called out to them.

Nodding, Aphrodite, Athena, and Persephone left the river and walked over to her. "Poor Alpheus," said Persephone who'd always been the most soft-hearted of the four goddessgirls. "No date. No girlfriend. And, without the cup, he's lost his newfound powers."

"Next time he tries a super-hard spell and it doesn't work, I wonder if he'll figure out that the cup was magic," Athena said. "Then he'll really be

kicking himself that he gave it back. Does make me feel a tiny bit sorry for him."

Artemis snorted. "I don't feel any sympathy for him at all! He tricked both Arethusa and me, so he deserved to be tricked in return."

"True," said Aphrodite as she and the others slipped on their winged sandals. "But I still don't understand why he was so desperate to go out with Arethusa and then you. And what did he mean by saying, 'I'm still me,' a few minutes ago?"

"Yeah," added Persephone. "And what was that happy dance of his about?"

"I was wondering the same," Athena agreed. "If you ask me, there's something fishy about that boy's behavior."

Just then the girls heard laughter. They turned to look toward the river. Alpheus and the slightly muddy

Karya were sitting on a patch of grass near the shore, laughing, while Chester leaped around them.

"Looks like Alpheus has already found another girl to like," Artemis observed. "One who actually might *want* to go out with him!"

Aphrodite nodded. "I predict a crush in the making."

"You don't need to be the goddessgirl of love to make *that* prediction," Persephone said.

The friends all laughed.

They watched as, unable to sit still for long, Karya jumped up to twirl. Then she sent another stick flying for her puppy to retrieve. "Good throw!" Alpheus called out to Karya.

Artemis grinned at the happy, goofy smile on his face.

# 13
## Together Again

**W**HEN ARTEMIS AND HER FRIENDS ARRIVED back at Mount Olympus Academy, they shucked off their winged sandals first thing. The minute they placed them in the basket by the door, any dried mud magically disappeared. After slipping on the sandals they'd left behind earlier, they started up the staircase to the girls' dorm.

"I *desperately* need a shower," Aphrodite said as they neared the fourth-floor landing.

"And my hair needs shampooing," said Athena.

"Ditto," said Persephone.

"There's nothing wrong with a little bit of dirt, but I feel absolutely *grimy*," Artemis admitted. "After I shower and wash my hair, I'll need to walk my dogs. Meet you in the cafeteria for dinner after?"

As everyone nodded, a grinning Athena elbowed Artemis. "Here's an idea," she announced. "After all you did today, maybe for dinner tonight you should treat yourself to a *hero* sandwich!"

Aphrodite and Persephone giggled and agreed wholeheartedly. "You deserve it, goddessgirl!" Persephone told her.

"Yeah, for sure," said Aphrodite.

"I don't know about that," Artemis replied, try-

ing to sound casual. "In the end, the nymphs solved their boy trouble themselves."

Her friends exchanged glances. "Ha!" said Aphrodite. "You may have fooled those nymph friends of yours, but we're your BFFs. We're not so easy to fool."

"You might even say we're fool*proof*!" Athena joked.

Pretending innocence, Artemis widened her eyes. "I don't know what you're talking about."

"Yeah, right," Persephone said. "We *know* you planted the idea in Arethusa's head to have Alpheus pick you out of a crowd."

"What? Really?" Artemis said in surprise. "I didn't think anyone heard me say what I did to Arethusa. Except for her, of course."

Aphrodite laughed. "Hello? I was standing right

next to you when you leaned over to whisper to her. I may not have Pheme's super hearing, but my ears work pretty well." After a moment, she added, "I don't think anyone else heard, though, if you're worried about that."

Athena nodded. "Yeah, and Aphrodite was careful to tell Persephone and me privately what she overheard you say."

Artemis grinned, and then shrugged. "I may have *planted* the idea, but it was Karya who first provided the *seed*—when she reminded me of Alpheus's pledge. And it was Arethusa, the other nymphs, and you guys who helped *grow* the idea into a plan."

"Wow," said Persephone. "I may be the goddess-girl of spring and growing things, but I couldn't have said that better!"

Everyone laughed.

"But seriously," said Athena as the girls hit the fourth-floor landing, "your actions really were heroic today, Artemis. Because true heroes exercise humility. They raise others up and give credit where credit is due."

*Athena's description of heroes is right,* thought Artemis. The next time she felt it was all up to her to solve someone else's problem, she'd remember her friend's wise words and her own wise actions today. Because by practicing humility and raising others up, she'd helped the nymphs to help themselves *and* her. "Thanks," she said. "And know what? I believe I *will* have that hero sandwich for dinner!"

The girls all laughed again. Then Aphrodite was pulling open the dorm door and they were all heading down the hallway to their rooms.

As usual, Amby, Nectar, and Suez couldn't contain

their excitement when Artemis entered her room. "Good to see you, too!" she said as they wagged their tails and leaped on her, sniffing the dried mud on her skin and clothing with interest. She gave them all hugs and ruffled their fur.

Then she walked past the beds to check that they still had plenty of food and water. For once she didn't have to pick her way around piles of stuff and risk stumbling over something. Looking around her room, she told her dogs, "I have to admit, our room has never ever looked this good before. Aphrodite's bin system really tidied things up! It's kinda nice."

After shucking off her borrowed gown, she tossed it over her shoulder onto the floor. "Oops, almost forgot. I'll have to get used to being neater!" She snatched up the gown and tossed it in the clothes

bin. Tomorrow she'd take Aphrodite up on her offer to magically clean it, since her own magical laundering skills were a little rusty.

Now Artemis grabbed her shower things and went down the hall to the bathroom. She had long ago perfected the art of quick showers, and so was in and out within minutes.

Back in her room, she rummaged through her quiver for the red chiton she'd worn prior to borrowing a gown from the nymphs. She'd been planning to put it on again, but then recalled that it hadn't been exactly clean when she'd plucked it from one of her clothes mountains that morning. And now, after being stuffed in her quiver, it was more than a little wrinkled. She took a sniff. *Hmm.* She deposited it in the dirty clothes bin, too.

Luckily, when she opened her closet, she found

the clean chitons that Aphrodite had salvaged during the big cleanup. She slid a dark purple one from its hanger. After slipping it on, she headed out the door with her dogs.

As they started downstairs, the sweet sounds of Apollo's kithara, a seven-stringed lyre, drifted down from the boys' dorm on the fifth floor. That was the instrument he played in Heavens Above. The song he was playing now was a pretty one, and it relaxed and pleased her to hear it.

She'd had enough of the river trail for one day. So instead of heading there, Artemis led her dogs toward the sports fields. Pulling their favorite bone-shaped toy from her pocket, she tossed it ahead of her as she walked. The magical toy zigzagged in the air a few feet above the ground, then bounced high

and then low. As usual, her three dogs tore after it, barking merrily. It would keep them entertained for a while without her having to throw it again.

Halfway to the fields, the toy made a superwide zigzag and splash-landed in a fountain. It was the one that the water nymph Minthe was now the caretaker of. Poseidon had designed it in the shape of a big O ring, in celebration of the most recent Olympic Games. At its center, water sprayed outward in loops and twists from the fountain's many spigots before tumbling into a mosaic-tiled pool below.

"Whoa!" said a godboy named Kydoimos. He was Minthe's new crush. He'd been sitting on the edge of the fountain, chatting with the green-haired girl, when the dog toy splashed down. He reached into the water and pulled the toy out.

"Over here, boys!" he called out to Artemis's dogs. Then he tossed the bone-shaped toy farther down the grassy slope that led to the fields.

"Wow, good throw, Ky!" Minthe told him in an admiring tone.

Kydoimos beamed at her. "Thanks."

Artemis was pretty certain that no one in the world but Minthe could have gotten away with calling him by a nickname. Kydoimos used to be quite a bully, but after meeting this pretty water nymph, he'd changed.

Seeing them so happy together, Artemis's heart ached. She turned away from the pair and followed her dogs down the slope. Actaeon had been so angry the last time they'd talked, she thought sadly. She wished she knew what was going on with him. Though she'd be heartbroken if he'd fallen out of

like with her, she'd get over it eventually. Like she had with Orion.

However, she knew that splitting up with Actaeon would hurt way, way more and for much, much longer. Orion had been an unworthy crush, but Actaeon was pretty much perfect, at least in her opinion. Until yesterday, he'd been sweet and funny, a good sport, and good *at* sports like her. Plus, he cared about her dogs, too. (Whereas Orion had only cared about himself!)

She was so busy mulling all this over that she didn't take much notice of the group of boys playing a ball game in the field ahead of her. Just then, her dogs stopped chasing after the magical bone-shaped toy. Abandoning it as it came to a rest in the grass, they raced toward the boys, tails wagging and ears flapping.

Artemis's first thought was that Apollo must be among the group, since her three hounds loved him nearly as much as they did her. But then she remembered that he was back at the boys' dorm, practicing his kithara. So that could only mean one thing. It was Actaeon they were heading for!

Sure enough, he emerged from the group with Amby, Nectar, and Suez leaping around him as laughter rang out from among the boys. "Later!" he called to his friends. After jogging over to the side of the field, he grabbed his schoolbag. Then, spotting Artemis, he trotted toward her with her dogs at his heels.

Artemis felt flutters in her chest as she watched Actaeon approach. *Ye gods!* In her eyes, this guy was sooo super cute! "Sorry my dogs interrupted your game," she said when he reached her.

"S'okay." He smiled at her so cheerfully before stooping to pet her dogs that she wondered if she'd only imagined his anger from the night before. Remembering his sharp words, however, and how he'd stalked off the archery field, she knew the anger had been real.

Finally, he stood again. "Can I walk with you?" A serious expression came over his face. "There's something I need to say."

"Um, sure," Artemis said. But her throat tightened with worry over what she might hear.

Her dogs ran ahead of them, picking up their bone-toy game again. Artemis and Actaeon followed more slowly, past the sports fields and the gymnasium, toward the edge of the Academy grounds.

Actaeon rubbed the back of his neck with the hand not holding his schoolbag. "I . . . well . . . I feel

like I owe you an apology," he said after a minute or two of silence.

This wasn't at all what Artemis had expected him to say. "What for?" she asked in surprise.

Actaeon paused, looking down at the ground. Finally he blurted out, "For the things I said to you yesterday. For my bad behavior when I stalked off the archery field like some spoiled brat."

"Oh," said Artemis. She waited for him to go on.

"I'd had a bad day," he explained, swinging his schoolbag as they walked along. "And I sort of took it out on you." He glanced over at her. Maybe to see how she was taking this?

She sent him an encouraging smile. "That's okay," she said. "I have bad days too. And sometimes when that happens, I also say and do things I'm sorry for later on." She hesitated for a moment, then asked,

"Did something happen at Game On!?" His mood had changed after his excursion there, she remembered.

He raised an eyebrow. "Have you been talking to Apollo?"

"No," said Artemis. "It was just a guess."

Actaeon sighed. "Your brother and some of the other godboys were on my team at Game On! yesterday. I got mad at them because they kept butting in during our game battles to save me from all the beasts. It seemed to me they only did it because I'm mortal. Like they thought I needed their protection."

"Oh," said Artemis when he'd finished explaining. "Well, Apollo really likes you, you know? I'm sure he and the other godboys would feel awful if they knew how you felt—"

"It's okay," Actaeon interrupted her gently. "When I finally got up the nerve this afternoon to tell him why I'd gotten mad, Apollo agreed that he and the others had been a bit overprotective. He said that in future game battles they'll only give me help if I ask for it." He grinned at her. "Then he added that it'll be my own fault if I die."

Artemis rolled her eyes. "Sounds like my brother, all right." The two of them laughed. They both knew that 'deaths' during any game battles at Game On! were simply pretend and totally harmless.

Gathering her courage, she asked, "So does it bother you that I'm an immortal and you're not?"

Actaeon looked taken aback. "Huh? No! I like that about you. Among other things. Lots of things. I mean, it's *you* I like." His face turned a little pink.

Overcome with relief at his answer, Artemis

momentarily failed to watch where she was going and stumbled over a small rock in her path. Actaeon caught her hand to keep her from falling. "Thanks," she told him.

"I may be a mere mortal, but I can make rescues too," he joked. Then he threaded the fingers of his hand through hers. "Speaking of rescues," he said, "how's it going with Arethusa and Alpheus?"

Artemis threw her head back and sighed. "Argh. Long story."

"That's okay," Actaeon told her. "I like long stories. But first . . ." Dropping her hand, he opened his schoolbag. "I made something for you," he said as he reached inside it. "Ta-da!" He pulled out the short, bright green arrow she'd seen him filing earlier at lunchtime.

He held it out to her. "Uh, thanks?" she said

uncertainly. Because what was she supposed to do with this tiny arrow? It was only about ten inches long!

Noting her dismay, he laughed. "It's not for target practice. It's a *directional* arrow. To keep you from ever getting lost again. And since it glows in the dark, you can even use it at night. I call it a GPS arrow—short for Goddessgirl Pointing System."

Hearing this, Artemis stared eagerly at the bright green arrow. "Really? How does it work?"

"Simple," Actaeon said. "You just tell it where you want to go and, step by step, it keeps pace with you, flying midair, and points you in the right direction. Like when you come to a crossroads, it'll point which way you should turn."

"Sooo cool! I could really use something like this!" Artemis exclaimed. "But how did you . . ." Her

words came to a halt. She'd been about to ask how he'd managed the magic to make the arrow, since he was mortal.

Unoffended, Actaeon smiled at her. "After I got the idea and made the arrow, I showed it to Apollo. I told him what I wanted it to do, and he cast a spell to give the arrow that magic. He said he couldn't believe he hadn't thought of the idea for you himself!"

"See? Mortals can do plenty of stuff immortals can't or don't think of," Artemis said, elbowing him gently. "I really, really like it. I'm sure I'll use it a lot!"

"You're welcome," Actaeon said, sounding pleased at her enthusiasm. "Now, tell me your *long* story. I'm kind of dying to hear it." He reached for her free hand, and once again they threaded their fingers together.

As they curved around the edge of the fields

and started back toward MOA, Artemis told him all about her two visits to see the nymphs and the river god. His outrage over Alpheus's trickery, the way he caused her arrow to miss what should have been a sure shot, delighted her. Because it showed that Actaeon cared.

"Alpheus was wrong, wrong, *wrong* to try to get you to take over Arethusa's promise to go out with him," he said in annoyance.

"You're right," Artemis said before going on with her tale. When she was almost finished, she broke off to say, "It was sweet of you to apologize earlier. But you were right about most of the things you said. When I tried to help Arethusa, I only made things worse. At least at first. Especially for myself! Then *I* was the one needing to be rescued!"

As they walked on, with her dogs still playing

catch with the bone-toy up ahead, she explained about the plan she'd thought of last-minute and then hinted at until Arethusa thought it was *her* idea. And about how Alpheus hadn't been able to pick her out from among the fifty cap-wearing, mud-spattered nymphs and goddessgirls. And how they'd temporarily turned him into a green mummy. Actaeon cracked up laughing as she described it all.

She was glad he was enjoying her story. "So I decided that in the future I won't be so quick to try to solve every problem for nymphs—or mortals, for that matter," she went on. "I'll try offering suggestions and guidance first. Give them a chance to see if they can solve their problems for themselves."

"I like your plan," said Actaeon. "And it sounds like Arethusa has proved she can come up with solutions too—under your guidance."

"Yeah." Artemis smiled, recalling how proud that nymph had been of herself for helping to solve her own problem. And she felt super grateful to her friends and all the nymphs who'd pitched in to refine and carry out the plan to foil the river god. *Helping others and* accepting *help are both good things,* she reflected.

"The strange thing is, my friends and I don't think Alpheus ever really cared that much about going out on a date, despite his trickery," she said now. "Athena said his desperation seemed fishy."

Actaeon looked at her with surprise. "Oh? Why's that?"

Artemis shrugged. "He just didn't seem all that upset when he failed to pick me out from among all those other girls." She paused to remember before going on. "Right after Persephone released him from

green-wrapped mummydom, he glanced up at the sky like he was checking the time. Then he shouted, 'Woo-hoo! It's five fifteen. And I'm still me!' And he did a happy dance."

She wrinkled her brow. "Weird, huh? I wondered if he'd been afraid the branches and vines Persephone had bound him with were going to permanently turn him into a plant."

Something flashed in Actaeon's eyes and he straightened. "Hey! You just reminded me of something! When I was with the guys at Game On!, I caught half a story Poseidon was telling about some godboy friend of his. The friend was about to turn thirteen, and Poseidon decided to pull a prank to, I don't know, *celebrate* it?"

"Totally sounds like something Poseidon would do," Artemis remarked with a smirk.

"Yeah. So, anyway, he told this godboy friend that just last week Zeus had decreed that from now on, every godboy on Mount Olympus must get someone to agree to go out with them—as in go on a *date*—before their thirteenth birthday. And this had to occur before the exact time of day they were born and in a public place in view of many of their peers. If not, Poseidon told this friend, they'd not only be losers, but they'd instantly and forever be turned into slimy slugs.

"He also said that no one was allowed to reveal to anyone the true reason they wanted a date." He shook his head. "Sounds dumb, I know, but Poseidon can be pretty convincing."

As she listened to this story, Artemis grew more and more excited. "That godboy friend he pranked

was Alpheus. Must have been! It makes total sense. I remember Arethusa saying he'd told her his birthday was *today*. The exact time of his birthday must have been before five fifteen this afternoon. So that's why he seemed mega-relieved when five fifteen arrived and nothing dire happened to him!"

"By nothing dire, you mean, he didn't start feeling *slug*gish?" asked Actaeon. Still holding hands, they both laughed like crazy.

"I guess Athena was right about his desperation being fishy!" Artemis said as soon as they calmed down. "Alpheus was set up by the godboy of the sea. What could *be* more fishy than that?" They both cracked up again.

Eventually, Actaeon said, "I can't believe Alpheus actually fell for Poseidon's dumb story. I mean, Zeus

makes a lot of decrees, but he'd never make one like that. He wouldn't want to put pressure on anyone to feel like they had to go out with someone before they were really ready."

"So true," Artemis agreed. She squeezed Actaeon's hand. She really, really liked this boy. "Speaking of *pressure*," she said before she could chicken out. "I don't want to put any on you, but would it be okay if I kissed you?"

A twinkle came into Actaeon's gray eyes. "No way!"

"No way, as in no way you want a kiss from me?" she asked in dismay. She dropped his hand and ducked her head back.

"No!" he said, his cheeks going pink. "I mean, no way I *wouldn't* want one."

Artemis smiled at him. Then, gathering her courage, she leaned forward and gave him a quick smack on the lips. Her first *real* kiss!

"Whoa!" said Actaeon. He grinned big when she pulled away. "I've only ever gotten dog kisses before. That was a *gazillion* times better!"

Artemis laughed. "Shh," she said, lowering her voice. "You don't want my dogs to hear you say that. It might hurt their feelings."

"Okay. We'll keep it our secret," said Actaeon. He looked and sounded happy. Exactly how she felt right now.

They linked hands again and headed toward the Academy. Maybe, just maybe, Artemis thought as they swung their hands between them, she was actually beginning to get the hang of this crush stuff!

# Authors' Note

**Artemis** (AR-tih-miss) is the Greek goddess of hunting, the wilderness, the moon, and wild animals. She is also the protector of young girls, just as her twin brother, **Apollo** (uh-PAH-low), is the protector of young boys. In ancient art Artemis was typically shown as a young maiden with an archery bow and quiver of arrows. Female nature spirits called **nymphs** (nihmfs) often accompanied her when she went hunting.

According to Greek myth, Artemis attempted to rescue the nymph **Arethusa** (ah-ruh-THOO-suh) when she was pursued by the river god, **Alpheus**

(AL-fee-us), who had fallen in love with Arethusa. In a different myth, Alpheus fell in love with Artemis, but she escaped him by covering her and her companion nymphs' faces with mud so he couldn't discover her. We kept both those myths in mind as we were writing this story!